An Anamorphic Game Called Love

by

Robin Winberg

An Anamorphic Game Called Love
Author: Robin Winberg
Copyright © June 2009

Manufactured in the United States of America

ISBN: 978-0-578-03067-8

Cover design by: John Petersen

1 Corinthians 13:1-8a and 13

If I speak in the tongues of men and of angels, but have not love, I am only a resounding gong or a clanging cymbal. If I have the gift of prophecy and can fathom all mysteries and all knowledge, and if I have a faith that can move mountains, but have not love, I am nothing. If I give all I possess to the poor and surrender my body to the flames, but have not love, I gain nothing.

Love is patient, love is kind. It does not envy, it does not boast, it is not proud. It is not rude, it is not self-seeking, it is not easily angered, it keeps no record of wrongs. Love does not delight in evil but rejoices with the truth. It always protects, always trusts, always hopes, always perseveres.

Love never fails....And now these three remain: faith, hope and love. But the greatest of these is love.

1 Peter 4:8
Above all, love each other deeply, because love covers over a multitude of sins.

Endless Thanks to my friend Eric Finnerty.

Chapter 1

Clutching my jacket together at the neck, I burrowed my face into the pseudo warmth as familiarity dictated my route home. My breathing became regulated as I chose to focus on the labor of expanding my lungs. It was only three blocks from where I worked, but it could be downright unbearable during the winter!

I dug my mitten covered hand into my mailbox, retrieving the days' correspondence. Most of the time, the only person who bothered to say anything to me went by the name of "bill".

Amongst the usual barrage of paper, something different had the audacity to show off. Squinting my eyes, I peered at the envelope, trying to deduce its origin and the nature of it. The return address said it was from a cousin on my fathers' side. Shrugging, I proceeded into my apartment and fumbled with the seal to reveal the contents.

"You are cordially invited to Robin Edwards' and Alan Winthrop's union…"

Sighing, I threw the mail down on a lone table next to the front door and meandered into the tiny corner kitchen.

"Mew." A soft squeak greeted me.

"Hey, Marie Rose. How was my girl today?" I smiled, scratching her behind the ears. She purred as she leaned her head sideways into my hand. She was a 7 week old gray tabby I brought home from the veterinarians' office that I worked at. I was her "foster mom", until she was old enough to be formally adopted.

Taking a look into the fridge, nothing appeared appetizing. And the thought of walking back into the frigid wrath of Mother Nature made me shudder. Shrugging to myself, I decided to take a bubble bath. I made my way into the narrow bathroom and reached for the hot water knob. The pipes shuddered into action as hot water spewed forth from the faucet.

As the water misted around the mirrored glass, the voice in the back of my mind told me I had to respond to my cousin's wedding invitation. My heart wasn't in it. Not that I didn't want to see her happy, but why did happy people feel it was necessary to remind everyone of it? Especially when those people were unable to find true happiness for themselves?

I stirred the bubbles and water around, checking the temperature. Marie Rose sat in the doorway, watching me as her tail sashayed back and forth. Slowly, I slid into the water and closed my eyes.

Why was I jealous of Robin? Was I jealous of Robin? Why was a part of me not happy to receive such wonderful news?

I absorbed a lung full of steam, mulling over all the thoughts and feelings that could possibly be stirring around in my soul. I was genuinely happy for Robin. I knew that her boyfriends in high school had been less than reputable characters, and that for her to consider marrying the guy she was engaged to meant he was a keeper.

My thoughts drifted to Michael, a man I had dedicated 4 years of my life to. We had our ups and downs like every couple, but in the end, our love wasn't enough to keep us together. He needed constant reassurance of my love (which manifested in such ways as calling me a dozen times in a single hour if I chose to hang out with any friend of mine), and felt his actions away from me needed no explanation (which meant if I had tried

to call him, he couldn't be bothered to answer the phone, no matter how

many days it had been since I'd seen him). And did he really honestly

think I approved of the "shadiness" of the characters he chose to keep as

company?

My heart ached at the failure of lost love. It's hard to invest that much

time and effort into someone and something, a cause that can't succeed

despite your best efforts. I had to learn all of the things I knew how to do

before Michael, like sleep without someone lying next to me, or not

having to share the bathroom in the morning, or not doing

laundry/cooking/cleaning/planning a life for two. Single town, anyone?

I listened to the sounds of silence, with the exception of Marie Rose'

delicate paws clacking against the hard wood floors. She wandered around

the tiny apartment, looking for a warm place to sleep. I could hear the

crinkling of plastic lining as she curled up inside my jacket. A good a

place as any, I supposed.

I looked around the bathroom, taking in the sudden abundance of

counter space. They seemed so white without any other color to contrast it.

There was only one light pink toothbrush, and Michael's aftershave no longer rested next to the cold water handle. The tub told a similar story, with only my expensive salon shampoos and conditioners to choose from, tucked in a corner. Michael's bargain buys were nowhere to be seen. He usually sprawled them all over the tub, even though he knew it aggravated me.

Eight months had gone by since I told him to get packing. Unbeknownst to me, he had been doing drugs (something I strongly disagreed with). I couldn't tolerate that, and I wasn't about to be lied to about his usage anymore. He knew the whole time how I felt, and he chose to deny partaking in those activities. He lied right to my face, until he failed a drug test for a prospective employer. So I kicked him out. Out of my apartment, out of my life.

I still missed his dark brown hair, his goofy smile, his hazel eyes, and the smell of his cologne… I missed everything. I knew I had made the right decision, but the consequences were still hard to bear.

Sighing again, I leaned my head back and drifted off to sleep. My neck stiffly bent around the frame of the tub as the heat from the water faded in waves of time.

Chapter 2

I could hear my cell phone echoing from somewhere through the haze, and it's shrill whine woke me from my watery nap. Stirring in the bath I could feel the icy chill the water had to offer, having exhausted its heat.

I shook my head, slowly reaching for the towel. I wasn't about to run naked through my cold empty apartment like a nutcase, just for a phone!

"Mew?" Marie Rose elongated herself as I reached into my coat pocket. Flipping open my cell phone, the inside screen showed the caller id. It was Sandy, a coworker of mine. I rolled my eyes and shut the phone. I could feel my temples pounding with mounting tension at the thought of listening to her hollow enthusiasm. For the past three months, Sandy had been trying to convince me to go out and meet people that Mr. Right was out there searching for me. The only catch was that we were at total odds about how to go and find him. Sandy believed that we "young people" needed to go to bars and clubs and various other places of that nature to find him. After all, I wanted a "fun man" who would make life exciting.

I was under the impression that there was no way I would find Mr. Right in a club or a bar or any place of that caliber. Not that there was anything wrong with those scenes. I just wanted a kinder, quieter man who didn't feel the need to party, a man who wanted to grow up and grow old with me. Maybe mature into the happy loving couple who spent their entire lives together, enriching each other throughout the years. I didn't think I was asking too much!

Sighing, I frigidly dried myself off and headed to the kitchen. I was going to make one more attempt in my efforts to find food.

My eyes fell as they gazed upon the dismal choices I had unintentionally offered myself. There was a half gallon of milk, a few eggs, some lettuce, and baking soda sitting on various shelves. Shaking my head, I slammed the refrigerator shut and headed off to bed. Marie Rose followed me, instinctively seeking out any warmth my small apartment had to offer.

My bedroom wasn't much, but it was mine. It seemed larger than it actually was since Michael removed his TV and dresser and sports paraphernalia. There was more space since he had taken his reminders.

Now there were empty sections in the room, leaving my mind to remember what the former remnants used to look like.

As we cuddled against each other under the comforters, her repetitious breathing brought me back to the land of the unconscious…

Chapter 3

"Good morning. Thank you for calling Happy Pets. This is Leslie. How can I help you?" I smiled into the phone. Regardless if the person on the other end of the phone was happy to talk to me, I loved my job. I couldn't help but be enthusiastic. Animals didn't lie to you the way people did. With animals, you knew exactly what they were thinking. If they were mad at you, you knew it. If they were hungry, they made you aware. When they wanted to love you, there was nothing you could do but surrender to the unconditional waves of affection.

"Hi, yeah. My dog is sick, and I'd like to schedule an appointment for her." A quiet masculine voice urged.

"Ok, sure. What seems to be going on?" I leaned my ear against my shoulder and removed a pen cap with my teeth. Eventually, he would need to schedule an appointment. Might as well be prepared!

"Well, we were watching football last night and I noticed her neck was swollen." His voice was hushed with panic.

"What do you mean, her neck was swollen? Like, her glands? Or her actual neck?" My eyebrows furrowed with confusion, trying to navigate through his unknowledged description.

"Her throat. Yeah, I guess her glands." His voice began to ease as he could sense the progress we were making at a diagnosis.

"Okay. Well, if her glands are swollen, she's going to need to come in and see a vet. What is the dog's name?" I poised the pen, ready to take action.

"Her name is Sera. She's a miniature Pomeranian. She's 3. I'm available all day. When's the soonest she could be seen?" Back to the urgency.

"Well, we have an opening tomorrow afternoon at 2pm. If you'd like, I'll let Dr. Tara know that you'll be stopping by." I smiled again.

"Sure, okay." He nodded.

"What's your name dear?"

"Sera."

"No, no no." I laughed. "What's your name?"

"Oh. Sorry." He laughed along with me. "My name is Jacob."

"Ah, I see you. You're already in our system!" I grinned.

"Yeah. You guys are good to Sera." He grinned back.

"Alrighty then. We'll see you at two o'clock tomorrow then."

As we exchanged our goodbyes, my heart broke a little. It was hard to be happy to people I didn't know when my personal life was in such shambles.

Chapter 4

"Hey stranger! I tried calling you last night! How come you didn't answer?" Sandy crinkled her nose at me and shook her head, and her cherub face widened even more as her short blond bob wildly waved back and forth. Sandy was one of those people who discovered the joys of college partying days and never grew out of them.

"Sorry. I fell asleep in the tub." I shrugged, offering a sheepish grin.

"Yeah yeah. You missed an awesome time at the club! It was insane! There was this wicked hot guy who offered to buy me shots. The only catch was he wanted them to be body shots!" Her whole face lit up like a child's on Christmas morning.

"Wow." I nodded my head forward once with my eyes opened wide, pretending to be interested. Did she really think this is the kind of guy I wanted to spend the rest of my life with?

"Oh, leave the poor kid alone. Can't you see that Leslie isn't interested in your shenanigans?" Alena scowled. Alena was the office mom. She may have been our age, but she had what people called an 'old soul.' Her behavior, tastes, and everything else ran parallel to someone from the Cold War Era.

"I'm just saying…" Sandy pouted off into a corner. My eyes looked at Alena with an enormous "thank you" flashing across them.

"What do you say baby girl? Lunch?" She smiled at me.

"Sure." Checking the clock, I could see her offer referred to the immediate future. Grabbing my purse, I waved goodbye to Sandy as Alena and I made our escape.

Chapter 5

Alena and I laughed over a glass of white wine as we picked at our salads.

"I know Sandy's just trying to help, it's just that I really don't think I'll find Mr. Right by going out clubbing every night!" I shook my head.

"I know, baby girl. Don't worry about her. Sandy's got a few screws loose. You do what you got to do, and don't worry about anyone else." She smiled at me.

"I know." I sighed; the weight of my breakup began to push down on my shoulders.

"Hey. Talk to me. What's going on?" She rubbed my forearm.

"It's…just…hard." My words were slow and labored.

"What's hard?" She continued rubbing.

"Well, for starters, how am I supposed to know Mr. Right when I see him?"

"Well, think about it. What qualities are you looking for in a man?" Alena half smiled at me.

"Huh, well... I guess I'm not sure." I furrowed my brows, contemplating her question.

"Okay. Well, let's start with the basics. You want him to not do drugs, right?" She asked.

"Yeah." I nodded, relaxing at the simplicity of her question.

"Do you mind if he drinks or smokes?" She continued.

"Not to excess, but no. I guess I don't care if he does every once in a while." I shrugged.

"Okay. What else?" Alena batted her eyelashes.

"I don't like being lied to." I spat, remembering Michael's countless stream of fictitious stories. "And I don't want to be called fifty million times an hour. And when I call, answer your phone!"

"Easy, killer! Talk to me. What's going on?" Alena leaned back in her seat, startled.

"Sorry. I just can't help but think of..." My voice trailed off, not wanting to confront the painful memories of a ruined flame.

"Ah, I see. Well, talk to me about it. 4 years is a long time to invest in someone, and I can't imagine that you would've stuck around if it was bad the whole time." Alena kept petting me. I was beginning to think she spent far too much time around animals!

"Yeah. There were good times, and there were good parts. But I don't know. I stuck around because I loved him. At least, I thought I did." I shrugged.

"What did you love about him?"

"Hmm..." I looked down, searching my brain for answers. "I guess I loved how he made me feel. He could make me feel special, like I was the only person on the planet when he was around." I smiled at the warm memory.

"What else?" She pressed.

"I don't know." I shrugged.

"Wow. That's it?" Alena's eyes opened wide with disbelief.

"Yeah, I guess. Why?"

"I was just wondering. What didn't you like about him? What did he do that upset you so much?" She munched on a forkful of lettuce.

"Oh my gosh! He did a lot! Let me tell you!" My words furiously began leaping off of my tongue, each more eager than its predecessor.

"Like I said, he would call all the time if I ever went out with my friends. I wouldn't have cared if he called once or twice, but he'd call like a dozen times in an hour! I'd have to turn my phone off if I wanted to have a decent time! If I did that, he'd show up wherever I was, and it'd be a fight! And I mean a huge screaming match that lasted for hours. But if I called him when he went out with his friends, he'd never answer. Sometimes, he was gone for days at a time. He'd never pick up the phone once! And it didn't matter how many times I'd bring up that point. He'd still freak out about me turning my phone off! If he couldn't find me, he'd call my mom and harass her about where I was! One time, he actually accused me of cheating on him, and he demanded that he be allowed 'to check for evidence'!" I shook my head in disgust.

"What? Are you serious? Check for evidence how?" Alena's eyes crumpled in confusion.

"Like he wanted me to strip naked and actually look for evidence, and he wanted to..." I motioned with my fingers, indicating a big no-no of my physical rights.

"Whoa! Are you saying he wanted to do a physical exam?!" Alena couldn't believe her ears.

"Yeah. I was like, no way. I went out and bought coffee. I have the receipt to prove it. I'm not letting you violate me because you're insane!" I shook my head. I could feel my eyes glaze over with raw seething anger. My right hand gripped the fork tightly, shaking with a fierce desire to smash something.

"Was there anything else? Or dare I ask?" Alena smirked at me. She knew as well as I did that there was more than enough evidence to indict Michael into the worst boyfriends of all time hall of fame.

"He told me the whole time that he didn't do drugs. If I ever had doubts, he'd go on a long tangent about how he didn't do that and he'd take a test to prove it and just because his friends did it, that didn't mean he did. And there was always people calling him! But he'd never talk to them around me. If I questioned his faithfulness, he'd flip out on me! One time, he had scratches on his back, and he said it was from playing basketball. Yeah, uh huh. Right." I rolled my eyes. "And he'd always say things that he knew would piss me off. It was almost like he was

deliberately pushing my buttons, <u>trying</u> to cause a fight!"

"Baby girl, that doesn't sound like love. Yeah, sure. Maybe you loved

him. But it doesn't sound like he loved you. If he really loved you, he

wouldn't have played games or put you through any of that." Alena gently

squeezed my hand. "Honestly, it sounds like he was abusive towards you."

"What? No. He never hit me." I shook my head emphatically. "He may

have grabbed my arm and dragged me, but it's because he wanted me to

leave with him."

"Oh honey. He was abusive. Physically, mentally and emotionally

abusive. He was definitely controlling. His insecurity and you constantly

having to cater to him, proving that you love him and you were faithful

and yada yada, that's abuse. He was taking more than he was giving. If he

really loved you, he wouldn't have lied to you or ignored your calls. I hate

to break it to you, but he was controlling and abusive."

My heart fell into an abyss. I was unable to mentally process her

truthful logic, not wanting to accept that I hadn't been able to see it for myself at any point in the relationship. I stared at Alena, experiencing a

loss for words.

"I can see why you're confused about love!" Alena laughed.

"Yeah, I guess so!" I laughed along with her.

"Come on. Let's head back to the office, and I'll explain to you what

love is." She summoned the waiter and asked for the check. After we had

cleared our lunch debt, we began walking down the street arm in arm as

she recounted her tale of true love.

"Baby girl, I was in a similar position to you. I dated a string of guys

who weren't right for me. Sure, some of them were good, but they weren't

right for me. So I decided to take a break from dating and concentrate on

myself. After giving so much of myself, I decided that I was important and

that I needed to pay attention to a person that I knew 100% that I was

going to have to live with. And I didn't want to be miserable. I wanted to

be happy. I also knew that I had to live with the consequences to my

actions, and that I needed to change how I behaved and what I thought if I

was going to be happy."

"I thought you were married." I tilted my head, getting lost by her story. Somehow, the facts weren't adding up in my head.

"I am. When I decided to improve myself, I started by going back to college for my veterinary assistant's degree. That's when I met John." Her eyes melted at the thought of her beloved.

"John's a good guy." I nodded in agreement.

"No, baby girl. John is a wonderful man, and I am thankful every day he's in my life. To be honest, if our marriage ended tomorrow, I would be grateful until the day I died for what he has given me." She smiled.

"Like what?" I winked at her.

"Oh, get your mind out of the gutter." I cracked up laughing as she playfully pushed me. Looping back around, our arms linked again as she continued her story.

"Like I was saying, John is absolutely wonderful. Because of him, I am a better person. Even if he wasn't around anymore for whatever reason, I will always carry him in my heart. Because of John, I have the courage to try any wild and zany idea. If it doesn't work out, it's okay. John has helped me to love myself, and accept myself for all of my quirks. He's also helped me to see where my limitations truly lie. Not the limitations that I thought were there, but the ones that were really there. I never thought I'd be able to get on the Dean's List at college! But John knew better. He knew I was smart enough, and because he was patient enough to help me through the tough classes, I ended up with a 3.8 GPA!" She kept smiling, daydreaming of her husband.

"Yeah. What else?" I pried, wanting to absorb as much of her knowledge as she could part with.

"A lot. It's hard to put into words, you know?" I could see her squinting her eyes, trying to articulate the words her heart had to say. "Well, for starters, John is always there. Whether I need him or not, he's always there for me. And he's infinitely patient with me. It doesn't matter if I say the wrong thing or what. He understands me, and he respects me. I can trust him. No matter where he goes or who he's with, I know he puts me first in his heart, and he would never do anything that could possibly affect me without discussing it with me."

"And he's always calling to say hi, or he loves me, or he heard a song on the radio or saw something that made him think of me. It's really cute.

One time, he was at the hardware store buying tools and he said he smelled my perfume. He said he looked around for me, but got sad when he realized it was another woman wearing it. He's adorable that way!" She smiled.

"Wow. I had no idea he was that wonderful." Stunned, I didn't really know what to say. Admittedly I was a tad jealous that she found her soul mate. But deep inside me, hope stirred. If Alena had been able to snag herself Mr. Perfect, then maybe I could find my own!

We entered Happy Pets with only a couple of minutes remaining in our lunch.

"You know we're not finished with this discussion, right?" Her voice was low. She meant business.

"Yes, mom." I rolled my eyes, shaking my head as I laughed at her.

"How about we finish it tonight over a cup of tea?" She grinned at me.

"Sounds fabulous. My place or yours?" I smirked.

"Yours. I'll walk home with you after work, and we will sort through all of this." She turned her back to me as she disappeared into the back office.

Chapter 6

I sat at the front desk, pondering over Alena's words. I never knew her to be a liar or a drama queen. When Alena spoke truthful words, sometimes they hurt. I knew in my heart she never intended to hurt me, but that was an unfortunate consequence of facing a demon I didn't know was looming in the shadows of reality.

It was very difficult for me to concentrate on the stack of papers sitting in front of me. I couldn't take my mind off of the fact that Alena was right. I had been abused. For four years, I had allowed myself to be a victim. How come I couldn't see it?

"What's the matter? You look down." Sandy pouted, wrapping her arms around me.

"Nothing. It's just a long day." I offered a weak smile.

"Maybe a drink would cheer you up." She grinned.

"Alena and I are having tea after work, sorry. Otherwise, I would." I grinned back. Maybe one of these days, Sandy would get the hint that I wasn't interested in partying every night.

"Well, whenever you want to come, you know my number. Besides, you'll never meet anyone just sitting around here." She shrugged, heading back to work.

"Yeah, I'll get right on that." I thought dryly.

Chapter 7

"Talk to me, baby girl. You've seemed upset since lunch. What's going on?" Alena blew into her purple tea mug, hoping to spare her delicate mouth from the seething heat.

"Oh, I don't know." I sighed, loosening my grip on my black mug. Alena was right. The tea was scalding hot!

"Well, something's going on. You've been in a funk." She twisted her lips to the side. Her inner guide knew there was a glitch inside me, but couldn't navigate around my soul to determine the origin of the problem.

"I don't know. I mean, it's hard to believe that Michael was abusive. I'm not saying you're a liar, but it's still hard to believe I didn't see it for myself, you know? What's wrong with me that I didn't see it?" I exhaled. Pity party for one, anybody?

"Hey now! There's nothing wrong with you! Just because you didn't see it, doesn't mean you're stupid or that you deserved it. Maybe he was a good con artist who got you to believe that he was a good guy." Alena spat in my defense.

"Then how am I going to find a good guy if I can't recognize abuse when I see it?" I shrugged.

"That's why I'm here baby girl. I want to help you find Mr. Perfect. We just need to sit down and analyze what qualities you look for, and what ones you're overlooking." She smiled at me.

"Okay." I hollowly smiled back. I wasn't sure who was going to make the first move sorting through this illogical mess, or how to even navigate.

"First off, you need to get over Michael. Yeah, I know. You spent four years of your life with him, and that's a long time to dedicate to someone, but things didn't work out. You need to let go so you can move onto the man you're supposed to be with." She darted her head forward once.

"That's easier said than done." I sighed.

"Why? Are you two still together? Do you still talk? What?" She shook her head, seeing answers.

"He calls every once in a while." I shrugged.

"And what does he say?" Alena leaned her ear towards me, indicating that she was willing to hear the ludicrous words that flowed from the once love of my life.

"Nothing worth listening to." I rolled my eyes, smirking.

"Then don't answer when he calls."

"I don't. Actually, I ended up calling the police on him!" I laughed.

"What? Why? What happened?" Alena jerked upright on the couch, nearly spilling her tea in surprise.

"He'd call and say things to deliberately piss me off, so I'd hang up. He'd keep calling and calling, trying to start a fight. So I had to call the police and get the police to tell him to leave me alone. Then he started coming to my apartment at like 2 or 3 in the morning! He'd be drunk or high or something and the only way to get him to leave were to call the cops! That's when they issued me an order of protection. If he 'bothers' me again, he goes to jail." I shook my head.

"Wow baby girl. I had no idea things got that bad!" Alena shook her head in disbelief with me. "When he called back, why didn't you just not answer?"

"Honey, trust me. If I didn't answer the phone, that's when he'd show up to my apartment. He left me no other choice but to call the cops."

"What a loser! I mean, seriously!"

"I know. So how exactly am I supposed to recognize Mr. Perfect when I couldn't see what a loser Michael was?" I sipped my tea.

"I understand. So how about we work on helping you identify Mr. Perfect?" She grinned at me.

"Sure. How are we going to do that?" I raised my left shoulder in question.

"First, we need to determine what kind of a person you are. Then we need to figure out what qualities you're looking for, okay?" She blinked, opening her eyes wide.

"Okay. What would you like to know about me?" I blinked back.

"Tell me your likes and dislikes." Alena sipped her tea, dipping her bag into the warm water.

"Well, I like animals. I don't like drugs. Um…" I trailed off, losing myself in my thoughts.

"You mentioned you don't like clubbing." Alena offered.

"It's not that I don't like clubbing. I just don't want to do it every day, like Sandy does." I wrinkled my nose in disgust. "I'd prefer to stay home and watch movies."

"Okay. Do you like to cuddle?"

"Yeah. Cuddling's fun." I smiled.

"Do you like shopping?"

"Not really. It's okay to do once in a while, but not all the time." I shrugged.

"Okay. Got it. Are you a religious person?"

"No, not really. I'm a spiritual person. I believe all things happen for a reason, but I'm not going to go to church. If there was a God, I highly doubt he or she would ask people to fight in his or her name." I shrugged again.

"True. You've got a point there. Okay, so no religious. I take it no fighting or violence or anything like that. What else? Are you athletic? Do you like athletes?"

"I like doing some things, but I wouldn't do them all the time. I like skating, football, walking, I don't know. I guess I like doing a lot of things, just in moderation."

"Gotcha. You're a sensible person." Alena pulled her left cheek up. "So what qualities are you looking for in a person?"

"Well, he's got to like animals. He doesn't necessarily have to own animals, but he can't be mean to them. And no drugs. I refuse to date someone who does drugs." I shook my head.

"What about prescription drugs?"

"That's a fine line with me. If they use prescription drugs for a reason, but they don't go overboard, then I guess that's fine. But if they're a zombie because they take too much, then no thank you. I'll pass."

"Okay. What else?" Alena set her empty mug on the coffee table, cracked her neck, and leaned back on the arm of the sofa we were sharing.

"Monogamy. That's a big one with me. I don't mind if he leaves for someone else. If I'm not making him happy, then he shouldn't stay and make me miserable. Don't get me wrong, it'd hurt like hell, but I'd rather him leave then the alternative. Besides, you don't know who has what out there! It seems like STD's are everywhere! And if I'm clean and I'm not cheating, then he shouldn't either!" I began to laugh with Alena.

"Absolutely. I totally agree with you."

"No stealing or racism. Those are big too. I've never stolen anything, and I've never said a racist word. I don't plan on it either." I shifted my weight, relieving my left hip bone of the pressure. I was careful not to allow any motion to disturb Alena.

"What about homophobic?"

"Duh. That's stupid." I rolled my eyes and snorted.

"Why's that?"

"First off, what do I care about what other people do with their lives? That's their business. They live with the consequences of their actions. I don't. I have no right to tell them how to live their lives, just like I have no right to tell straight people how to live their lives. By the same token, people don't have any right to tell me how to live my life. If I live with the consequences of my actions, then it's up to me to decide what actions are necessary. Don't you think?"

"No. I meant what about dating a homophobe?" Alena corrected herself, smiling at my tangent.

"Oh. No, absolutely not. I'd hate it. The only race that makes mistakes is the human race. I can't stand it when people target a single group for whatever stupid reason. Like I said, if you don't like it, then you don't have to do it." I hissed. Nothing got me worked up quite like politics!

"Besides, if you can still go to bed at night knowing there are people out there in the world you disagree with, then you're fine. I don't know why people get uppity about other people doing things that are different from them. If you don't like it, then walk away and don't do it yourself. It's as simple as that. I mean, seriously…"

"Okay. What about dating women?" Alena grinned.

"What?" I wrinkled my face, not understanding what she was getting at.

"I'm just saying, have you ever thought about dating women?"

"No, not really. I just don't find them attractive. I like men. Plain and simple."

"Okay. Just checking." We shared a good laugh. "Do looks matter? Or let me guess. In moderation, right?"

"Yep. I don't care if he's a little chubby or a little skinny or a little muscular. Just nothing too extreme."

"Well, that's good."

"What's good?"

"That your main focus is on personality. I'll tell you what, baby girl. It seems to me that a lot of kids nowadays are focusing on the outside package, and dissolving the relationship when they find something they don't like about the inside package. You should settle down with someone because of who they are on the inside, not the outside." Alena closed her eyes briefly.

"Besides, if there's something wrong with the outside, then go to a plastic surgeon and fix it!" I cracked up laughing.

"Oh, you're horrible!" She threw a pillow at me.

"I'm just playing. I don't mean it. Besides, my mother always said 'Pobody's Nerfect'."

"Don't you mean Nobody's Perfect?"

"Same thing."

"Alright, baby girl. I'm getting tired. I think I'm going to call it a night. How about we go out for lunch tomorrow, and I'll narrow down the list of candidates for you?" Alena stood up and stretched.

"Sounds like a plan. You know I love you, right? What would I do without you?" I smiled, wrapping my arms around her.

"I don't know, but you won't have to find out baby girl. I'll always be here for you." She reciprocated the physical gesture.

"Sisters?" I asked.

"Sisters. 'Till the end." She smiled.

Chapter 8

The next day, I eagerly searched around for Alena. I was like a child watching the clock at the end of any and every school day, dying to go to lunch with her.

The night before I had begun to relax under a mound of plush comforters as Alena's words sunk in. Maybe Michael was a good con artist. Maybe that's why I didn't see it. That didn't necessarily mean I was a bad person who deserved it.

I was perfectly content diving in the mound of paperwork that discouraged me the day before. Going paper by paper, the pile began to slowly shrivel into nothingness as order burst through its former chaos.

"Um, hi. I have a two o'clock appointment." A gentle voice startled me, bringing me back to the present from my own little world.

Looking up, the room began to blur around the man standing in front of the counter. He was the only thing that my eyes could focus on. It was as if everything faded off into the background, and we were the only two people in the world. Somewhere in the back of my mind, I was vaguely aware of reality occurring, but I couldn't take my eyes off of this marvelous creature! His light green eyes were so kind and gentle. Without realizing it, my soul was being consumed by the wonder of the man standing in front of me.

"Welcome to Happy Pets. How can I help you?" I numbly replied. My brain couldn't comprehend his magnificence and work related duties.

"Hi. I called yesterday about my dog Sera. I scheduled a two o'clock appointment." He smirked, revealing a beautiful dimple.

"Oh yes! Hi! How are you?" I smiled back, flipping the book sitting on the front desk open to the notes I had previously made. "Where's Sera?"

"She's right here." He blinked, continuing to smirk at me.

Leaning forward in my chair, I looked for a dog. I could see a leash in his hand, but I couldn't see the animal that was supposed to be on the other end of it.

Furrowing my brows, he bent over and retrieved the smallest bundle of fur I'd ever seen!

"Ruff!" Sera squeaked, seizing in his arms. She was so excited to see another human being that she was desperately trying to jump to me.

"Oh my goodness! She's so tiny!" I reached for her.
Gently, we made the exchange. As my hand brushed up against his, my entire nervous system went haywire with electric impulses as every hair on my body stood up on end.

"Yeah. She's really miniature. I'm sorry. I should've warned you that Sera was tiny." He batted his eyes at me, and I could feel my cheeks flush under the scrutiny of his gaze.

"According to her records, she weighed 2 lbs 5 oz when she was here last month for her vaccines." Sera had found an imaginary spot of dirt on my cheek and put all her might into removing it with her tongue. "Oh my gosh! You are so cute!" I cooed. "Well, let's get her into an exam room, and I'll let Dr. Tara know you're here." I handed him back his 'squeaky toy come to life' and headed down the hall. Tall, dark and gorgeous followed closely behind.

Once we reached an empty room, I smiled as I slowly closed the door. My heart thumped wildly as I shook all the way back to my chair. Who was this man, and why did he have such an effect on me?

My head remained in the clouds for several moments, long enough for Sandy for sneak up on me unnoticed.

"Hey, girly!" She grinned ear to ear, wrapping me in a giant hug.

"Hey." I replied, jumping slightly at the surprise of her touch.

"I'm sorry. I didn't mean to scare you." She laughed.

"No, you didn't. I'm just trying to get through this paperwork." I shook my head, trying to wrestle free from the emotional clouds hanging onto my soul.

"Yeah?" Sandy peered over my shoulder. "Have you told Dr. Tara that she has a patient?"

"I suppose I should." I blushed, picking up the phone.

"You mean, you haven't told her? What's going on?! It's not like you to space out!" Sandy's eyes opened wide with surprise. She was a dog with a scent, unable to determine the origin. She knew something was amiss, and Sandy was the kind of nosy busybody to not let go without the full scoop.

"I have no idea." The words floated out of my mouth, my mind drifting back to the intoxicating handsomeness of the man with the miniature dog.

"Well, I'll go let Dr. Tara know for you. Then we can talk." She refused to let her canary eating grin fade from her cherub cheeks.

"About what?" I looked up from my paperwork, locking eyes with her.

"I didn't know if you wanted to do something tonight." Sandy's left shoulder brushed up against her left ear as she blew me a nonchalant kiss.

"We'll talk about it." I smirked back at her, rolling my eyes. One thing you could say about Sandy. She was definitely persistent!

As I was left alone with paperwork and thoughts, I couldn't help but wonder how this man had been able to stop time. Why did a complete stranger have such power over me?

Chapter 9

"I told Dr. Tara. She's with the patient now." Sandy sauntered back over to me.

"Isn't that the smallest dog you've ever seen?" My nose crinkled in delight.

"Oh my goodness, yes! I can't believe how tiny she is!" Sandy smiled back. "Did you check out that total babe walking the dog?"

"You mean the owner?" I asked.

"Yes! He's a total babe!" Her face lit up in excitement.

"I didn't notice." I lied. "I was interested in the patient."

"You can't honestly tell me you didn't notice how absolutely gorgeous he is!" Sandy's eyes opened wide in disbelief. "You should see if he's single."

"What?" I laughed. "I don't think so."

"Why not?"

"I don't think I'm his type."

"Says who?"

"Trust me." I rolled my eyes.

"Trust me. Why not give it a shot? It's not like you're meeting Mr. Right. Why not try for Mr. Right Now?"

I rolled my eyes again, shaking my head. Where was Alena when you needed her?

"So, are we going to go tonight or what?"

"Where do you want to go?" As if I needed to ask.

"Well, there's this new club down on Main Street..." Her grin turned sheepish. She was incorrigible!

"How about we go out Saturday?" I offered a compromise.

"Why Saturday?" Her face contorted in confusion.

"I can't come to work with a hangover!" I laughed.

"Suit yourself. Hey look! There he is!" Sandy's voice dropped to a hushed whisper.

"Hello, again. So what did Dr. Tara say?" I smiled as the handsome stranger with the adorable dog returned.

"She said that Sera has an infection and a couple of bad teeth, so she's going to need blood work done and surgery." His voice was feathered with sadness as he stared at the floor.

"Aww. Don't worry. We'll take care of her." I beamed.

"I know you will." He smiled, looking up at me.

As our eyes locked, we were both spellbound by the unspoken magnetic force that drew us into one another. I wondered if he felt it, too.

"What are you doing Saturday?" Sandy piped up, breaking the silence.

"I'm not sure. Why?" He asked, his eyes darting over to her.

"Leslie and I were talking about going out for a drink. Do you want to come?" She smiled.

"Leslie? That's a nice name." He smiled at me. I blushed.

"So is that a yes?" Sandy beamed.

"We'll see." He smirked. "When should Sera come in for her blood work?"

"Well, we have an opening Saturday at noon. How does that sound?" I thumbed through the appointment book, scanning availability.

"Sounds like a date!" Sandy piped up. I gritted my teeth. I couldn't want for this handsome stranger to leave so I could smack her!

"Sounds good." He reached for a card propped upright on the counter and scanned it. "Who do I call in case Sera has an emergency?"

"Oh, here. Let me give you Leslie's number." Sandy reached for the card before I could interject. As she scribbled it down, I just offered a light smile and a shrug at him. He shrugged back, indicating our helplessness when it came to Sandy.

"This is Leslie's cell phone number. Call anytime if you have any questions about animals." Sandy smiled as she returned the newly acquired information.

"Will do. I'll see you Saturday." He smiled at me as he turned and left.

Once the door had closed, my eyes flashed in disbelief at Sandy.

Chapter 10

"What?" Sandy smirked at me. She was so dense. Sometimes, I just wanted to reach up and slap her!

"I doubt I'm his type." I rolled my eyes.

"You never know especially if you don't ask." She grinned.

"What's going on?" Alena furrowed her brows as she entered the conversation. Her arms were carrying bags of kibble and boxes of needles.

"Sandy's giving my number out to every guy who walks in here." I exhaled, looking at Alena.

"Are you serious?" Alena nearly dropped her supplies in surprise as her eyes bulged out of her head.

"You should've seen the way Leslie looked at him!" Sandy raised her hands in defense.

"Still, you don't do that. You don't give out someone else's information. That's rude." Alena scolded, setting the kibble down.

"I wasn't trying to be mean." Sandy pouted, skulking off.

"The sad thing is she's right. She wasn't trying to be mean. She was just trying to help." I sighed to Alena.

"I know she was, baby girl. But you're right. How do you know that you're his type? Did he seem interested? Is he single? There's a lot of factors involved in this scenario. Just because Sandy likes to socialize with people doesn't mean you do." Alena lectured.

"I know, but she was just trying to help." I sighed again.

"Did he seem interested?" Alena pried, a dimple peeking out of hiding in her face.

"I don't know. A little bit, I guess." I shrugged, trying to analyze the events that had transpired.

Alena placed the boxes of needles in the desk drawers, and pulled a chair close. "Well, either he did or he didn't."

"I don't know. The whole thing was weird." I looked Alena in the eyes, unable to explain the unusual spiritually cosmic response.

"Weird how?" She tilted her head at me, not clear of my meaning.

"Well, his name is Jacob, and he had the smallest little puppy you've ever seen!" My words tumbled out as my body jumped up in excitement.

"Seriously, Alena. She was so cute! She was this big!" I spaced my hands a foot apart from each other. "And she was really fluffy, with reddish fur."

"Uh huh, okay. What about him?" Alena raised an eyebrow at me.

"Well, he's really quiet, and he seemed genuinely concerned about his dog…" I began.

"Was he wearing a wedding ring?" She inquired.

"Not that I recall." I shook my head.

"Did he smile?" Alena grinned.

"Yeah."

"Did he look you in the eyes?" Her face was lighting up in increments.

"Yeah." I blushed, tilting my face into my shoulder to hide the sheepish grin.

"Did you look him in the eyes?" Alena leaned closer as her excitement began to mount.

"Of course."

"Any sparks?"

"Huh?"

"Were there any sparks?" Alena began petting my arm.

I blushed, unable to think of what to say. My eyes darted, wildly looking around for the right words. How could I articulate such a cosmic connection?

"Oh my gosh! There were! There were sparks!" Alena jumped up in her chair, squealing with delight.

I just sat there, unable to process her giddiness as she jumped up and down with her arms wrapped around me.

"Oh baby girl, I'm so happy for you!" Alena couldn't have been more excited. The question was why wasn't I? Was I missing something? Or were they making more out of this than there really was?

Chapter 11

I wandered aimlessly through the grocery store, staring absently at the items placed on the shelves. I had always been picky when it came to food. My recent break up (okay, maybe not <u>that</u> recent) had left my spirits down in the dumps, not able to regale in grocery shopping.

I decided to head down the junk food aisle, a place I knew was bound to yield somewhat fruitful results. Even though potato chips weren't the healthiest thing I could put in my mouth, it was better than nothing. Usually I feasted on lean meats, veggies, and fruits. And by feast, I meant graze. I was a grazer. I grazed all day long. I never really got full, but I was never really hungry.

At 5'8" and 130 lbs, I had a long lean frame to show for my nibbling. I was what most people called "petite", although I wasn't unnaturally thin. I was one of those people who wouldn't be caught dead in the gym. I had light brown hair, hazel eyes, and average features. Let's put it this way. I wouldn't have stuck out in a crowd. I'd be able to blend in with everyone else, not receive a second glance, just come and go about my business like the insignificant spec that I was.

I stared blankly at the potato chip section, drifting off into space, when my insignificance popped up on someone's radar.

"Hey. Leslie, right?" a hushed whisper greeted me.

"Huh? Yeah. Oh hey." I snapped back to reality, following the sound of my name. It was Jacob, that really cute guy from my work! He was still wearing a fitted gray sweater over a pair of jeans. His blond hair was tousled perfectly, allowing his bright greenish blue eyes to peer through the strands.

"Sera, right?" I stuttered. My heart fluttered into my throat as I struggled to speak.

"Sera's my dog." He laughed.

"Oh, I'm so sorry!" I started laughing.

"It's Jacob." He smiled.

"Hi Jacob. How are you doing?" I smiled back. He had a really nice smile, warm, inviting...

"I'm alright." He peered into the empty abyss that consisted of groceries I had placed in my shopping cart. Looking up, his eyes crinkled at me. He was so cute!

"I know, I know." I rolled my eyes. "I need to eat a better diet than nothing."

"To each their own." Jacob shrugged with a grin. He had a couple bags of potato chips in his hands.

"I suppose." I smirked with a shrug. I absently looked around the aisle, and decided to abandon my junk food quest. With Jacob around, I couldn't concentrate on what food to fill my fridge with.

"So, how long have you worked at Happy Pets?" Jacob inquired.

"About 7 years. I started just before I was 18. I love it there."

"What about that girl who was with you?" Jacob asked.

My heart sank. Was he asking me about Sandy because he was interested? Oh, please! I hope not!

"Sandy?" I threw the word out there, as if her name had suddenly become a curse word.

"Yeah. What's with her? Is she always so... odd?" He shook his head.

"Oh. Yeah." I laughed with relief. "She's always doing things like that. She's constantly trying to get me to go out and party and club and drink and hook me up with any and every man she can. Don't mind her." I waved it off.

"Ahh. I see. And here I thought I was special." He snapped his thumb against his middle finger.

"You're special!" I blurted out, turning red at the realization that I had unintentionally started nibbling on my foot. Too bad I wasn't in the condiment aisle!

"Well, thank you." He laughed. "How come a wonderful person like you is single?"

"Long story." I rolled my eyes.

"I've got time. How about we put food in your cart, and you can tell me all about it?" Jacob smiled. My heart fluttered.

"Let's just say I learned the hard way that I don't know a single thing about love." I wrapped my fingers around the handle. "What about you? Are you single?"

"Yes I am." Jacob blushed.

"How come?" I furrowed my eyebrows playfully at him. How could a wonderfully handsome, charming guy like this be unattached?

"I guess I haven't found the right person to settle down with. I dated around when I was in high school, but I don't want to casually date. I want to meet my soul mate and settle down, I guess." He shrugged.

"I hear that!" I nodded, grinning.

"Well, I'd better get going. I have my nephew's birthday party to go to. Everyone's going to wonder why it took me so long to buy chips!" He laughed. "I'll see you Saturday though, right?"

"Saturday?" I stared blankly, trying to recall any mention of the word during our long grocery trip.

"Sera's blood work?" Jacob asked, wiggling his head.

"Oh yeah! At noon. I remember. Speaking of, I don't know how much knowledge you have about Pomeranians and their health. I know quite a bit, if you'd like a crash course." I smiled.

"Sounds great. How about coffee after her blood work?" He shifted his weight from his left foot to his right.

"Sure." I smiled.

"Alright. I'll see you Saturday then. Have fun." As his fingers scrunched goodbye, the nerves in my intestines rippled upwards as millions of butterflies' wings crashed in my stomach.

Chapter 12

The coffee pot percolated as I paced profusely across my small kitchen floor. I had excitedly called Alena, and she promised to rush right over so we could squeal over my small victory.

During the several hours I'd been at the grocery store, I managed to walk away with a head of lettuce, a bottle of creamer, one quart of rice, and a gallon of milk. I was going to have to go back and give shopping another go if I was going to survive!

"Hello hello, baby girl!" A voice chirped through the front door. I skipped over to the entryway and flung the barrier to the side, inviting Alena into my arms.

"Hey Alena!" I buried my face in her hair, inhaling the scent of her peach shampoo.

"So what happened?" Alena twisted her arms behind her, trying to remove her jacket.

"Okay. So I went grocery shopping, and I ran into him!" I bubbled.

"Him who?" She looked at me vacantly.

"Jacob." I stated, opening my eyes wide. The look in my eyes told her she should've known, and the look in her eyes replied she was clueless. "The guy with the mini pom from work?"

"Oh. I didn't hear about this. Do tell!" She smiled, reaching for a coffee mug.

"Okay. So this guy came into work with a miniature Pomeranian saying her glands were swollen, and he was so cute!" I giggled. My mind began to spin as the memory of his aura engulfed me, and I willingly succumbed to its appeal.

"That's it? He was cute?" Alena wrinkled her brows in confusion.

"No, of course not." I shook my head. "So anyways, Sandy was a total freak and gave him my cell phone number! You know, just in case he 'had questions about his dog', because he couldn't call the doctor, or whatever."

"Well, I ran into him while I was grocery shopping, and he is so cute! We're going to have coffee after his blood work this Saturday." I grinned, feeling my cheeks burn.

"Oh, I remember talking about this. I thought you said this was earth shattering." Alena frowned.

"It is!" I nodded insistently.

"How so?" She raised an eyebrow at me.

"Honey, you should've been there. It's so hard to describe. I was sitting there at work, minding my own business, when he came in. And when I looked up... I don't know. It's hard to explain." I shrugged, wrapping my soul in the warm fuzzy feeling that came with remembrance.

"Are those stars in your eyes?" Alena squealed, perking upright.

"Maybe." I smirked, blushing.

"Oh my goodness! You have to give me all the details! Come on! Start spilling!"

As time slipped away from us, I carefully laid out the details of my dual encounters with Jacob, how the room had slowed down, how even Sandy didn't annoy me when he was around, and how I had no idea what it meant or how to act or anything. It was almost as if he cast a spell on me, rendering me mentally incapable of everything.

"Sounds like it could be the real thing." A mischievous grin appeared from behind the rim of her coffee mug. "So you admit now that there were sparks?"

I just rolled my eyes in response.

Chapter 13

Most people wouldn't have such a difficult time deciding what to wear when it came to work. Dress codes dictated what options were available. How could I make myself look attractive while following the strict guidelines? Was it even possible?

I decided to focus on the other qualities that represented me, like my hair and moisturizer and whatnot. It was my feeble attempt to maintain some control over my appearance, desperately trying to fight back the inadequacy the hospital scrubs left me with. Offering the mirror an encouraging smile, I spun on my heels and walked off to meet my destiny.

I felt like I was walking on the moon as I bounded down the sidewalk heading to work. I could've floated away on the cloud of ecstasy that surrounded my feet. My heart fluttered inside my chest, unable to escape, unable to stay put. The anticipation of seeing Jacob had cast an unusual spell on me, and I had no choice but to surrender to its effects. What was it about this guy that had me all in knots, that made me incapable of behaving normally? Was Alena right? Could Jacob really be the one?

Only time would tell, but how much time? Would I know immediately?

Or would I have to wait another four years before I knew the truth?

Chapter 14

Every now and then, my eyes shot a dirty glare in the direction of the clock. The seconds refused to tick by at a decent pace as I was forced to wait for destiny to come and meet me with its latest update. I tried to focus on the paperwork and pending appointments. When even a part of you is preoccupied with something else, anything else, going about your daily habits can be the most arduous task of all!

I was so consumed with trying to distract myself that I was oblivious to the fact that it had actually worked. I didn't even hear Sandy and Alena sneak up on me.

"Hey baby girl. Working hard, or hardly working?" Alena smirked at me.

"Oh, hey! I didn't even see you two there." I smiled back. "I'm just trying to get through this paperwork."

"Seems like all you do is paperwork." Sandy pursed her lips at me.

"You do what you got to do." I shrugged. "It's called work. And what are you two doing?"

"Nothing really. We have one appointment today, so we're just waiting to do blood work." Sandy grinned at me. My heart began thrashing wildly at the hint of Jacob and his beautiful eyes.

"Shut up. His dog is sick." I rolled my eyes at the indication of 'magic in the air', but it was no use. Alena and Sandy kept smiling away.

"Aren't you two going out for coffee afterwards?" Alena teased.

"Yeah. I offered to give him inside info on small dogs. I'm just trying to be helpful." I shook my head a little.

"Uh huh. And are you this helpful to everyone who comes in with a little dog?" Sandy shot.

"If they asked for help, sure." I shot back.

"How come you offered it to him instead of having him ask for help?" Alena asked.

I sighed. These two were not going to stop until they heard what they wanted. I just shook my head and returned my attention to my paperwork.

"Aww sweetie, we're not trying to upset you." Alena rubbed my shoulders.

"Yeah, we're sorry. "Sandy wrapped her arms around me.

"You guys are making a big deal out of nothing." I grumbled, aggravated by the discussion.

"We just want what's best for you, and he seems like a really great guy." Alena followed Sandy's example and continued the group hug.

"Besides, it sounds like there might be a genuine spark." Sandy squeezed.

"There might be, but only time will tell. Until then, there's no point making a mountain out of a molehill." I flexed my arms upwards to encompass theirs, completing the group hug.

We all heard a familiar bell as the front door opened. I could see Jacob through Alena's blond hair that had fallen in front of my face.

"Aww. What a great moment. Too bad I left my camera at home." Jacob smiled.

My heart fluttered once again upon seeing Jacob's dimples. His soft features lulled my soul into a peaceful sense, leaving me feeling warm, fuzzy, soft, safe, and secure. I could feel my inner core being pulled into his essence, and I knew resistance was futile.

"Hey stranger!" Sandy squeaked.

"How's the puppy doing today?" I fumbled with my tongue. Leaning forward, I could see a feisty ball of fur dart around the office as she absorbed all the scents we had to offer.

"She's good. There are moments where she just wants to rest, but for the most part, she's an active spaz." Jacob laughed as we all watched her get tangled in her leash.

"Well, how about I take her and we get started on her blood work?" Alena offered, loosening her bear hug grip around my shoulders. Without a word, Jacob relinquished Sera over to Alena and we watched them disappear around the corner to the lab area.

I looked over at Sandy, wondering whether she was going to stick around or excuse herself. Without missing a beat, Sandy resumed her naturally clueless nature and began chatting with Jacob about her clubbing excursion the night before. I couldn't help but roll my eyes at her obliviousness.

A blood curdling screech electrified the air, paralyzing everyone's vocal chords. We looked around in silence, unsure of our next move. The only sound that radiated through the animal hospital was the announcer from the TV in the waiting room, rattling off the weather forecast.

Moments later, Sera and Alena appeared from behind closed doors. We all waited for an explanation.

Even a blind person could see the changes in Sera. She was no longer full of energy, eager to experience everything life had to offer. She was shaking viciously, traumatized by the forceful penetration of the needle into her fragile tiny leg. Her eyes beckoned sympathy from all onlookers, pulling everyone's heart strings.

"Aww, my poor little pooch. Did the needle upset you?" Jacob's hands floated up and Sera's little body wriggled, eagerly trying to obtain Daddy's comforting embrace.

"So, how about that coffee? I'd love to hear what you know about Pomeranians." He asked from behind a mound of fur licking his face.

"I get out of work in an hour. Is that okay?" I asked, my heart sinking an inch.

"Oh, don't be silly baby girl. We got you covered. Go enjoy your coffee." Alena stepped forward, nudging me towards the door with her shoulder.

"Are you sure?" I tilted my head at her.

"Absolutely. Pet care is what we're all about at Happy Pets!" She smiled, nodding her head towards the exit.

"As long as you don't mind…" I shrugged.

"Not at all. You just have that pile of papers to do, right?" Alena's eyes opened in search of answers. I knew she was secretly telling me she'd want to hear all about my "date" when it was over.

"And inventory." I replied.

"Gotcha. Have fun." She waved, disappearing behind the receptionist area.

"Let me get my coat." I threw over my shoulder to Jacob. He seemed unfazed by the delay, relishing the reunion between him and his beloved pet instead.

I walked towards him with my coat in my left hand and my purse in my right. "Shall we?" I smiled.

Jacob and I approached the door, setting out to meet our destiny that awaited on the other side…

Chapter 15

Jacob returned from the cash register with a cup of coffee in each hand. "I don't know how you take your coffee. I hope it's okay." He sat down across the table from me.

"Cream, no sugar." I smiled.

"There's sugar in it. Do you want me to go back and get you a new cup?" Jacob pushed his chair backwards, bracing his legs to bear his body weight.

"No no no. That's fine." I put my hand up, shaking my head.

"Are you sure?" He furrowed his brows.

"Yeah, it's fine." I smiled. He smiled back, the tension in his shoulders visibly easing.

"So…" He looked up from his steaming latte.

"So, what would you like to know?" I smirked.

"Everything!" Jacob's face lit up, relieved from his fishing duties. I get the feeling he was not the type of guy to pry for information.

"Well, Pomeranians tend to live 14 to 18 years." I began. "However, there are several factors that affect their longevity." I blew on my coffee, watching the steam swirl around in the air.

"Like what?"

"Well, it depends on how often you get them their shots, and what you feed them, and if you regularly take them for walks, and things like that." I sipped, wincing a little. I wasn't used to sugar, and this cup was definitely sweeter than I preferred.

"It is too hot?" Jacob shot upright, detecting my flicker of discontent.

"No." I pulled the corners of my mouth down, shaking my head.

"Are you sure?" His forehead and eyes crinkled, unsure of whether or not to believe me.

"Yeah." I nodded. My short term memory drew a total blank. "Where was I?"

"You were talking about the factors of health." Jacob filled in the missing memory pieces.

"Oh yeah. Thanks. Like I was saying, it depends on what you put into them. Dogs and people are like machines. If you perform proper maintenance and provide the right fuel, there's no reason you can't extend their life."

"I feed her puppy kibble. Is that okay? I know she's not technically a puppy anymore, but she's so small." Jacob's eyes sought approval.

"Small kibble is fine for a small dog. Eventually, you want to find small adult kibble instead of puppy kibble. And no more table scraps!" I lectured, my eyes beaming the "I know what you've been doing" glare.

"I don't!" He protested.

"Don't lie." I laughed. "I know Pomeranians' mouths have crowding and their prone to infection, but at 3 years old, it was accelerated by a diet of table garbage!"

Jacob looked at the floor, a sheepish grin revealing his adorable dimples. "You're right. You got me."

"I wouldn't recommend a person eating that garbage! Don't feed it to a poor animal!" I wagged my finger at him, returning his grin.

"Hello, Jacob." A snotty, squeaky voice shot. We looked up to meet a pair of glowering brown eyes.

"Hi Dana." Jacob's voice had a hard edge as he responded to this foreign woman.

"On a date?" Dana hissed. Her body was rigid as she stared down at our cups of coffee.

"We're just talking about proper pet care." I shrugged.

"Dana, this is Leslie, Sera's vet. Leslie, this is Dana." Jacob mumbled.

"Hi. It's nice to meet you." I reached my hand outwards, offering a peaceful shake.

"Hi. We used to date." She hissed, wrapping her venomous claws around my hand.

Her words slapped me in the face. Unable to blink, breathe, or respond in any capacity, I just stared and let her jerk my hand in a vertical motion.

Jacob rolled his eyes. "We went to the movies a couple of times. It was no big deal."

"Well, I'm glad to see you've found someone new." Dana pulled her cheeks upwards, but her eyes continued to throw icy daggers at everyone sitting at the table. My peripheral vision conspired with my inner core, both of them trying to distract me from the uncomfortable nature this foreign woman had bestowed upon our conversation. It felt like every single nerve ending all over my body was being caressed by a white hot needle as an invisible machine applied increasing pressure to my lungs. What I wouldn't have given to fade away into the icy cold breeze outside.

"Like I said Dana. This is Leslie, Sera's vet. We're having a conversation about pet care over a cup of coffee. You're welcome to sit and chat with us." Judging by Jacob's tone, he was quickly losing patience with Dana's roaring jealousy.

"Thank you, but I have a ton of errands to do. Give your parents my regards." Spinning on her heels, she continued on her own personal warpath as we watched the back of her fade into the moving crowd on the sidewalk.

My brain was still spinning, left to process the information that was just presented to it. And I knew beneath the surface, there were questions and feelings swirling around. However, I wasn't able to grasp them or organize them. When it comes to matters of the heart, logic usually goes right out the window.

Was Jacob still the wonderful guy my soul interpreted him to be, or was he just another jerk trying to pass himself off as a decent guy?

Chapter 16

I just stared at Jacob, waiting for him to initiate some sort of conversation. The passing seconds intensified the awkwardness of the situation, and his eyes radiated a powerful softness towards me. I could feel myself being pulled into him as he manipulated time.

"So Dana..." I nodded. "She seems... interesting." I shrugged, unsure of the ground I was treading on.

"Yeah, interesting." Jacob's disapproving tone shot his words out with the ire Dana had bestowed upon the mood.

"I wonder why things didn't work out." I nodded in sympathy, secretly trying to pry for information.

"Because nobody wants to date a jealous control freak!" He burst out into laughter, his beautiful eyes crinkling at the corners, revealing their inner light. It was captivatingly awesome!

"Seriously? I just thought she was a bit of a bitch." Leaning in, I whispered the treacherous words in a hushed whisper.

"Yeah. She'd call me up and ask me if I wanted to go see a movie. She meant to ask if I wanted to watch the movie she wanted and pay for it." He rolled his eyes. "Besides, Dana's not my type."

"Because she's controlling?" I smirked, my eyes opening slightly in innocence. I was hinting at a desire for him to express interest, but the hint appeared to have gone over his head.

"That's part of it." His left cheek wryly slinked upwards, revealing one lone dimple.

My heart fluttered at the shrouds of mystery surrounding his words. I couldn't help but hope he was somehow referring to me.

I did a quick check of his body language. Jacob was still perfectly perched around his coffee, his firm right hand wrapped around the cup. Not a flicker from anywhere on his body. Nothing. Was he interested in me?

"So, what were we talking about before?" I asked, trying to distract myself from the disappointment.

"I believe you were lecturing me on what I feed Sera." Jacob laughed. The corners of his eyes crinkled again. He was so cute!

The feelings of connected joy came rushing back to me, before that unwelcomed stranger had ruined our 'date'.

"Right. Okay, you can't be feeding her table scraps. I know she's cute, and you want to make her happy, but animals are a lot like small children. They need an adult to set boundaries. You wouldn't let a three year old stay up past midnight eating candy watching scary movies, would you?" I resumed my rant.

"Maybe." Jacob teased. He glanced up from his coffee cup and our eyes locked.

As the afternoon hours walked towards the iridescent hues offered by the setting sun, Jacob and I continued to build the foundation surrounding our own little world from the rest of existence. The only mystery cloaking us from society was in which context?

Chapter 17

"How was your date yesterday?" Sandy scrunched her face at me. Her eyes lit up with anticipation of juicy details that were to never come.

"It wasn't a date. We went out for coffee. He just asked me a few questions about proper pet care." I shrugged, rolling my eyes.

"Did he pay or did you go Dutch?" She tilted her head.

"He paid." I looked up at Sandy as she started squealing.

"He paid?! Then it was a date!" Sandy clapped rapidly.

"You are such a dork!" I shook my head and laughed at her.

"Why aren't you happy? You met somebody!" Sandy grinned.

"I made a new friend. We're not dating." I replied, my heart dropping an inch at the truth. I couldn't very well ask Sandy to play scout, could I?

"Why not? Is he a bad kisser?" Sandy whispered, leaning into my ear.

"What? No! I mean, I don't know!" I stammered.

"Do you like him?" She poked my cheek with her nose. She was always an odd girl!

"Yeah, I guess." I blushed slightly, burrowing my face into my nurses' smock.

"So then ask him what he thinks of you." Sandy poked me again.

"I can't do that!" My voice softened.

"Why not?"

"Because."

"Because why?" She sure was insistent!

"Because I can't." I exhaled loudly.

"Fine. Then I will." Sandy stood up, arching her shoulders back. She had a strange serene smile on her face, almost like she thought she was delivering me from lonely solitude.

"What? Why?!" I whined.

"Do you like him?" She folded her arms across her chest.

"Yeah, I guess." I slowly shrugged, unable to organize my feelings.

"Okay then." Sandy sauntered away, not giving me a chance to continue my protests.

Sighing, my hand shook as I reached for a file. Things were no longer in my control, and I was helpless to play the hand I would be dealt. I knew

Sandy had my best interests at heart, but I wondered how much of her

head would dictate the conversation. What would she say to Jacob? How

would he react? Would Jacob be receptive to the idea of being in a

relationship with me, or would he laugh at the idea? Did I want this door

opened, or would the consequences be too much to bear?

Chapter 18

The rest of my work day was shredded to kibble, my mind unable to focus on anything but Sandy. She wasn't known for her grace, and I worried about her word choice with Jacob.

Since our chat, Sandy's presence had become a figment of reality's imagination. Only Alena and I were left to run the office.

Her maternal instinct must've told her that something was wrong because she kept looking at me and frowning.

"What's wrong?" I asked, wrinkling my forehead.

"Funny. I was about to ask you the same thing." Alena copied my facial expression.

I sighed. "Nothing."

"Then why don't I believe you?" She put her hands on her hips.

I just sighed. I knew she was right, but I wasn't sure of what to say or how to say it.

"C'mon, baby girl. Spill. What's up?" Alena plopped herself in a wheeled chair and scooted herself towards me.

"Sandy said she was going to talk to Jacob." My voice barely came out above a whisper.

"Why?"

"Because I guess I kind of like him, and Sandy's trying to hook us up." I shook my head.

"What business is it of hers?" Alena was still puzzled. Sandy's logic train had a way of only having her for a passenger.

"It's not. I think she thinks that you're not complete unless you have a man." I looked up at Alena, trying to read her.

"So how do you feel about him?" She asked.

"I do like him, yeah. I think he's a great guy, but I'm not in a hurry to rush into anything." I stated.

"What do you know about him?"

"Like what?"

"What does he do for a living? Where does he live? What are some of his hobbies?" Alena threw her questions at me like darts.

I sat back in my chair, speechless, my eyes slightly bulging. She was absolutely right. What if Jacob was a nice guy, but he engaged in questionable activities? I didn't know a darn thing about him!

"I have no idea." I admitted.

"Sounds like you should take more time to get to know him." Alena nodded.

"What about Sandy?" I inquired.

"I'm sure that no matter what she says to him, you can blow it off as the nonsensical ramblings of a party girl." She rubbed my back.

"True. You're the best, Alena." I smiled at her.

"I love you too, babe." She smiled back.

Chapter 19

Marie Rose and I were cuddling in bed together, enjoying the quiet and the stillness of the night. No words were exchanged. Just the mutual love between a cat and her human.

I listened to her breathe as thoughts swirled around in my head. Despite my fiercest efforts, they hounded me, driving me to the edge of insanity. What was Sandy going to say to Jacob? How was he going to react? What was Sandy going to reveal about my feelings? I couldn't help but worry how this was going to play out.

A shrill pitch shattered the silence as Marie Rose and I simultaneously jumped. Sleep clouded her small brain as she looked around for an answer, and I leapt out of my warm cocoon towards the noise.

"Hello?" I flipped open my phone, rushing it towards my ear.

"Hey. Did I wake you?" Jacobs' gentle voice greeted me, and my heart went wild.

"No, no. I was just hanging out with Marie." My voice shook as the air escaping my lips trembled.

"Oh. If you're busy, I can let you go." Jacob said.

"No, no. I'm not busy. What's up?" I asked.

"I thought you said you were hanging out with someone."

"Marie's my cat." I laughed.

"Oh." Jacob laughed with me. "Okay. Now I don't feel so bad."

"So what's up?" I reiterated.

"Nothing. I got a weird phone call from one of your coworkers." I could hear him smile.

My gut tightened against the imaginary fist Sandy had thrust into it. "Oh yeah?"

"I think it was the one who wanted you to go drinking with her." Jacob stated nonchalantly.

"Sandy?" I asked.

"Yeah, I think so."

"So what did she have to say? Or dare I ask?" I laughed nervously.

"Oh, just stuff."

"Well, would you like to come over and talk about it? I mean, you don't have to if you don't want to." I stammered. Why did he make me so nervous?

"Sure, I guess. Where do you want to meet?" He was always so calm and cool about everything.

"How's my place?" I shrugged. I wanted to see his body language and reactions, two things I couldn't do over the phone.

"Okay. Where do you live?" He asked slowly.

As I gave him the clearest directions I could, I ran around my room looking for suitable attire. While I didn't mind if Sandy or Alena saw me in my pajamas and slippers, I wasn't about to let a prospective suitor see me at anything less than my best.

Chapter 20

I ran a wet hand through my hair, trying to revive some life into my lifeless straw. My heart continued to pound. I wasn't sure what I was most nervous about. What Sandy could've possibly said to Jacob, his reaction to what was said, or how he felt. All I knew was that I needed to roll a snake eyes on only one of those categories and it was game over for this possible romance. Besides, a part of me was hesitant. I barely knew him, but there was something drawing me to him. It was an inexplicable phenomenon.

I threw my shoulders back and straightened out my shirt. I had decided to go with a gray t-shirt with a kitten on the front and a pair of hip hugger blue jeans.

I carried my shaking petite frame into the front foyer and waited to hear the doorbell or a knock, some kind of noise to indicate his arrival.

The wait seemed forever as I started wandering around, nitpicking every detail of the arrangement of the furniture. The same shrieking pierce broke the silence, and I jumped.

"Hello?" I exhaled into the phone.

"Hey. I'm here." Jacob's cool voice replied.

"Rock on. I'm coming." Hanging up the phone, I looked around for Marie Rose. I didn't need her escaping into the frigid cold outside. When I thought the coast was clear, I opened the door an inch.

"Hurry." I urged, whipping the door open and pulling him inside.

"Okay." He started laughing. "I don't get it."

"Sorry." I let go when we were both inside. "I just don't want Marie escaping."

"Ahh. That makes sense." Jacob shook out his arm.

"Purr?" Marie Rose ran into Jacob's leg, trying to butter him into reopening the door.

"Oh wow. She's so little!" Jacob marveled.

"Yeah." I agreed.

"How old is she?" He bent over, trying to scoop her up into his arms. Marie's antisocial nature took over as she ran under the couch.

"Just over seven weeks. Sorry about that. We found her on the street abandoned. I'm trying to make her more sociable so she can be adopted, but she's still a bit shy." We both peeked under the sofa to see a pair of day glow eyes staring back at us. I couldn't help but smile.

"It's okay. Sera was like that when I first brought her home. She'd run and hide under everything. It took her awhile to warm up to me." Jacob smiled back.

"So..." I could feel my heart wildly begin to thrash. "You talked to Sandy?"

"Yeah." Jacob nodded. He appeared to be slightly nervous as well, almost as if he had slightly curled into himself as his eyes fell to the floor.

"What did she have to say?" I inquired.

"Well, she was asking me things like if I was interested in you and if I was a good guy and if I was going to treat you good and stuff like that." His voice was hushed.

I had two seconds to think of the perfect response. "That's Sandy for you."

Jacob's eyes rose up to meet mine. "What do you mean?"

"Oh, she's always trying to hook me up with someone or get me to go to the bar and meet 'Mr. Right.' " I laughed. "I swear, she's only interested in 'Mr. Right Now.' Not saying that you're a bad guy or anything. I just don't know anything about you." I smiled at him.

"Well, what would you like to know?" He returned my smile.

"What am I allowed to know?" I smirked.

"Anything you want." He smirked back.

"What do you do for a living? You know where I work. Where do you work?" I asked, heading towards the kitchen.

"I work at Apples and Oranges as their lead technician." He responded as he followed me.

"That computer place?" I dug around in the cupboards for all the tea I could find.

"Yeah. I've always loved computers." He put his hands in his back pockets.

"Would you like any tea?" I asked, showing off my various bags.

"Sure." He pointed to the orange pekoe box.

"What are some of your hobbies?" I asked, putting his teabag in a mug.

"I love swimming. I volunteer at the youth center as their lead lifeguard on the weekends." He smiled at a warm memory.

"Aww. Would you like milk or sugar?" I asked.

"Sugar's fine. What are some of your hobbies?"

"Oh. Um, I like cooking I guess." I shrugged. "I'm not sure. I work a lot."

"Okay, so you're a workaholic." Jacob laughed. "I am too."

"Rock on! That's another thing we have in common." I smiled as I handed him his tea.

"What's the first thing?" Jacob furrowed his brows.

"We love animals." My left cheek went up.

"Oh yeah." He smiled, revealing two beautiful dimples and that twinkle in his eye that melted my heart.

"And we're both single." I headed towards the living room where several seats awaited us and flopped on the biggest couch.

"Yep." He flopped down a cushion away from me.

"How old are you?" I asked.

"27. How old are you?" He responded.

"24. What's your longest relationship?" I blew on my tea.

"2 years, but it wasn't really a relationship. All we did was go to the movies once in a while, and we didn't kiss or anything. It was like hanging out with my sister. How about you?" It was his turn to hide behind the steaming mug.

"4 years." I exhaled loudly, trying to push the memory of Michael away with the air.

"That's a long time." Jacob looked up at me.

"Yeah."

"How come it didn't work out?" He asked.

"Turns out he was a good liar, but I caught on to all of them." I rolled my eyes.

"Like what?" He really wanted to know. I wasn't sure why, or how much I should divulge, but I knew this could work in my favor.

"For starters, he did drugs. And I don't. And he knew how I felt about drugs. He'd hide using from me. He also cheated on me, a lot. After a while, I had had enough and I called it quits." I looked at my tea bag, fighting back the anger and pain.

"Wow. I'm sorry." He shook his head, confused.

"Not your fault. I just wish I'd known sooner so I didn't have to waste four years to figure out he was a total jackass." I took a sip.

"Yeah, I know how that feels. I kind of feel like I wish I hadn't have wasted two years with Dana. Don't get me wrong, she's not that bad of a person. We're just not compatible."

"Yeah, you said at the café she wasn't your type." I nodded in agreement. "So what is your type, if you don't mind me asking." I looked up at him and smiled in hope.

"Uh…" He stammered, caught off guard. "Um, I'm not sure. I guess I don't really have a type."

"Oh, come on! Everybody has qualities that they look for or avoid. What are some of yours?" I laughed, throwing a pillow at him. Lucky for him, my aim was horrible as it completely missed.

"Well, I don't like drugs either. That's another thing we have in common. And I don't like cheaters. I say if you're going to cheat, don't waste my time. Other than that, I don't really care if a person's tall, short, skinny, fat, or what." He reached for the pillow, and gently tossed it back over to me. "What's your type?"

"Crap." I thought to myself. "How much detail should I give him?"

"Um, well, I like blondes." I blushed a little.

"Oh yeah? Is that why you noticed me?" Jacob laughed, roughing up the golden mess on top of his head.

"Of course." I grinned.

"Okay. What else?" He grinned back.

"Well, drugs are a definite no-no. And he's got to be monogamous, and he's got to have a job." I stated matter of factly. "And he's got to be nice."

"I'm surprised you don't have a preference in eye color." He teased.

"I do, actually. I prefer blue or green eyes." I teased back, wrinkling my nose.

"What about bluish green?" Jacob cracked up laughing. I didn't see what was so funny.

"Sure. That works too." I smiled back.

"I'm sorry. I have a dorky sense of humor." He wiped a tear from his eye. I seriously didn't see what was so funny.

"It's okay. I have a warped one." I shrugged.

"What do you mean, warped?" Jacob took a breath.

"Like when I'm watching a horror movie, and someone predictably jumps in the audience. I start cracking up." My eyes opened wide as I smirked.

"Ahh. I see." He opened his eyes wide in response. I opened mine even wider. Pretty soon, we were both pursing our lips at each other as our eyes bulged. That caused us to crack up laughing. It felt good to laugh with someone.

"Purr?" Marie Rose asked, cautiously approaching Jacob.

"Hey, little missy. Felt like coming out of hiding?" He wiggled his fingers at her, beckoning her to come. She complied, but in a playful manner.

"Oh!" Jacob jerked his hand back as he realized Marie Rose had brought her claws out to play.

"Sorry. I forgot to tell you that she isn't declawed yet. The appointment is in a few weeks." I pouted, feeling guilty.

"It's okay. She just caught me off guard."

"I have another question." I perked up. I couldn't believe I had forgotten to ask this one.

"Shoot." He sipped.

"Are you the aggressive or passive one in the relationship?" I grinned.

"Ha. Definitely passive. How about you?"

"Definitely aggressive." I nodded.

"Yes sir!" He saluted, and we both started laughing again.

"I got a question for you." His words were softly spoken, as usual, with little vocal inflection to go on.

"Shoot."

"Are you interested?" Jacob asked. His words were slow and careful.

"In what?" I wrinkled my eyebrows at him, but my gut knew what he was getting at. That's why the air caught in my throat.

"In me, I guess." He shrugged.

Crap. How was I going to answer this without sounding weird or desperate or ruining the wonderful moment we were having?

"A little. How about you?" I threw the ball back in his court, desperately trying to avoid any embarrassment.

"Let's put it this way. I wouldn't be opposed to the idea." He smiled at me.

"Rock on." I smiled back, blushing.

"So how does this sound? We could take things slow, at first. Until we're both comfortable. There's no reason to rush into anything, right?" He continued to smile. I loved looking at him smile.

"Right. That's absolutely true." I continued to smile. I couldn't help it.

"Actually, I have a confession to make. When Sandy called me up, I thought she was asking me out for you." He blushed.

"Oh yeah?" My eyebrows arched, searching for more details.

"Yeah. I was kind of hoping.." he let his words trail off into the small space between us.

"Hoping what?" I tilted my head to the left.

"That you were interested." Jacob reached across the couch cushion that separated us and gently wrapped his hand around mine. He was soft to the touch as thousands of nerves tingled with anticipation. My heart fluttered at the connection.

As we looked into each other's eyes in silence, I could feel my entire being melt...

Chapter 21

I tell you! I was on cloud nine every day for the next week! Every little thing made me smile. Even when Sandy began pestering me for details, I didn't get upset.

"Oh, come on! He didn't say a word to you about it?" Sandy whined. She was dying for information.

"I told you, he only told me that you called and that he thought you were asking him out for me." I repeated, sighing. I didn't want to openly discuss mine and Jacob's decision, in case things didn't work out.

"And?" Sandy nudged her head forward.

"And what? We talked." I moved my left shoulder vertically.

"About what?" Sandy was beside herself with curiosity and ignorance. What a perfect trio!

"About everything. Where he works, what he does for fun, past relationships, yada yada..." I said as I pulled a file folder off of the desk and opened it. Hopefully, Sandy got the hint that this discussion wasn't open for discussion.

"Uhh! You're impossible!" Sandy stormed off.

"What was that all about?" Alena scrunched her face as if she'd nibbled a lemon wedge.

"Remember how I told you Sandy was going to call Jacob on 'my behalf'?" I asked, looking up at her.

"Yeah?" Alena slowly handed me her response.

"Well, Jacob called me to talk about it, and one thing led to another, and…" I began.

"Oh my gosh, baby girl! You didn't!" Alena's hands flew up to her mouth, her eyes wide with fear.

"No! We didn't do anything. We just talked." I leaned in and whispered.

"Oh, thank goodness!" She threw her grateful arms around me.

"What would make you think that?" My mind couldn't wrap itself around what would make Alena think I would behave like that.

"I know Sandy does that, and that's her choice. I just worried that since she got involved… Anyways, you were saying?" Alena took a deep breath, offering a hollow smile.

"Like I was saying, we talked and we have decided to take things slow." I genuinely smiled.

"Oh baby girl! I'm so happy for you!" Alena offered a real one back. "But how slow is slow?"

"That's a good question." I scrunched my forehead, trying to come up with an answer.

"Well, I do have this for you." Alena handed me a folder.

"What is it?" I scratched my scalp, looking at the nonsensical charts inside.

"The results of Sera's blood work. She does have a slight infection, and she's going to need a week's worth of antibiotics before we can clean her teeth. You're going to have to call Jacob and let him know." Alena winked at me, grinning.

I looked up at the ceiling for a split second. These girls were incredible!!

"Okay. I'll let him know. What kind of medicine do you recommend?" I asked.

"I'd probably go with a small tablet, and have him wrap it in a little bit of wet kibble. Make sure she takes it every day!" Alena warned, wagging her finger at me.

"Okay." Instinctively, I reached for the phone. This time, my nerves made me pause. I couldn't help it! I was so nervous. I mean, we had just agreed to "take things slow." I hope he didn't think I was a loon stalking him!

The phone rang after I tapped in the numbers. Part of me desperately wanted to hear his voice. Another part of me wanted to hear his voicemail.

"Hello?" Jacob's beautiful voice answered.

"Hey. It's me." I smiled into the phone.

"What's up?" He asked, returning my smile.

"Not much. Do you have a couple of minutes?" I nibbled on my lower lip.

"Not really. I'm having lunch with my mom." His voice took on a sad note.

"Oh. Okay. I was just going to go over Sera's blood work results with you."

"Oh! Then, yeah. I have time. What's going on?" He suddenly sounded concerned, the same tone I heard when he'd first called me.

"Well, I guess she has a slight infection, and she's going to need to take antibiotics every day for a week to clear them up. We can't clean her teeth until the infection's gone. If you'd like, you can pick the tablets up any time today. I can help you go over the instructions when you get here, if you'd like." I smiled, hoping he'd rush right over for his beloved ball of fur.

"Okay. When I'm done with lunch, I'll swing by." He smiled.

"Okay. See you then." I smiled, my heart doing a back flip.

"Bye."

"Bye." And so the wait began...

Chapter 22

Every time the door opened, I practically leapt out of my seat in anticipation. Of course, it never was Jacob. But I'd only hung the phone up approximately 10 minutes ago. Hell, for all I knew, he could take an hour for lunch!

"So, what did he say?" Alena asked.

"He said that as soon as he was done eating lunch with his mother he'd come by and pick up her antibiotics." I relayed the information to her.

"Okay." She nodded slowly.

"So where are they?" I laughed, looking around for their unmistakable container.

"Right here." Alena dug her hand in her lab pocket and retrieved a small brownish cylinder. "The instructions are on the label."

"Thanks, babe. You're the best!" I smiled.

"I love you too, baby girl." She smiled back.

The familiar bell sounding caused both of us to look to the door. There he was. My new beau!

"Hey. Welcome to Happy Pets." I smiled as he sauntered up to me. I assumed the older woman who was with him was his mother. She dressed fairly conservatively for a woman her age, and she always walked upright. She didn't appear to have that much makeup on, but she did overdo the jewelry aspect (in my opinion).

"Hey. You called?" Jacob smiled back. I wasn't sure how to act around his mother, or if he'd told her about us. I wasn't going to act on our new founded relationship on the off chance he hadn't delivered the news to her yet.

"Yep. Sera's antibiotics are right here. Give her one tablet a day for 10 days, and then we can clean her teeth. In fact, you can schedule the appointment now, if you'd like." I smiled.

"How about we wait and see how she's feeling afterwards?" He kept smiling. I wanted to jump up and wrap my arms around him, but fear kept me seated.

"Okay. That works. Just make sure you put the tablet in a little bit of wet kibble. That way, she won't know it's there and she'll eat it." I winked.

"Ahh, I get it. Outsmart the dog. I got it." He winked back.

"Jacob Walters! I hardly think that behavior is appropriate! Do you?" His mother lectured, giving him a glaring eye.

"Relax, mom. We're friends." Jacob put his hands up in defense.

"Then why haven't you introduced us?" She folded her arms across her chest.

"Mom, this is Leslie. Leslie, this is my mother Noelle." Jacob waved sideways.

I extended my hand. "Nice to meet you." I smiled.

"Nice to meet you, too. Tell me. How do you know my son?" Her grip was firm.

"Through Happy Pets. He brings Sera here." I smiled. I was determined to make a good impression!

"Ahh. I see." She nodded.

"Yeah. They're all really good to her here." Jacob winked at me while his mother's back was turned.

"Well, we should be going. Your father will be wondering what's taking us so long." In a huff, she briskly headed towards the exit.

"It was nice meeting you!" I called after her. Waving to Jacob, he held his right thumb and pinkie next to his ear as he pointed at me with his left index finger. I nodded, indicating I'd wait for his call.

Taking in a deep breath, I could only wonder what his mother would think about the two of us dating. She didn't seem so thrilled at the idea of us being "friends". I couldn't imagine her being giddy at us being closer than that. Then again, why did he introduce us as "friends"?

Chapter 23

Once again, I struggled with an empty cart as I sauntered up and down every grocery aisle. I was trying to run errands to keep my mind busy until Jacob called me, but all I could think about was him. I had so many questions for him! I kept checking my phone. No missed calls. No new text messages. I just sighed and continued pushing the cart.

Shrugging to myself, I began to think. *I don't know what I'm getting all antsy about. He's not Michael. He's not playing the games Michael played.*

Yeah, but why wouldn't he introduce you as his girlfriend to his mother?

Maybe it has something to do with taking it slow. I shrugged. I hated feeling like I had an angel and the devil's advocate on my shoulder, constantly arguing.

A shrill whine distracted me from my torn feelings, and I gladly welcomed the interruption.

"Hello?" I sang into the receiver.

"Hey babe! What's up?" Sandy sang back.

My heart dropped. That was not the voice I wanted to hear.

"Oh, not much. Just grocery shopping. How about you?" I tried to hide my disappointment.

"Nothing really. Just getting ready to do laundry so I have some cute clubbing outfits for this weekend! Interested?" She voice lilted.

"Maybe. We'll have to see." My vocals chords mimicked her enthusiasm.

"Oh yeah. Might be doing something with the man." She laughed.

I rolled my eyes, getting ready to throw a witty retort her way when the call waiting beeped. It was Jacob.

"Hey, babe. Let me call you back. I have a beep." Without waiting for a reply, I clicked over.

"Hey." My heart could barely handle the swarm of butterfly wings that had sprung forth to life from nowhere.

"Hey. Sorry about earlier. I didn't get a chance to tell you that my mother can be a handful." He sounded slightly sad.

"It's okay." I responded slowly.

"Is something wrong?" He was quick to pick up on my disappointment.

"Not really. I was just wondering why you introduced me to as a friend." I walked over to the yogurt section, and started to scan for a few delectable goodies.

"Oh, that. I just didn't want to hear her complain. She never approves of anyone I date, and I just didn't want to hear her two cents." Jacob's voice rang with an aggravated tone.

"Ahh. I see. I was hoping that's not what you meant by 'taking it slow'." I laughed.

"No." He laughed with me. "I just meant no sex."

"Ahh. Gotcha." I could picture his sweet face turning red at the "s" word.

"Is that what you meant by taking it slow?" I asked.

"Kind of, yeah. I don't know. I mean, I'm not really sure." He laughed again.

"Okay. That really helps." I laughed.

"Sorry." He was so cute!

"So what are you doing?" I asked.

"Nothing really. Just getting ready to go watch a hockey game with some friends. How about you?"

"Grocery shopping." I shrugged with my left shoulder. I had managed to find my favorite yogurt and put several in the cart.

"I wish you more luck than last time!" He grinned.

"Thanks." I smiled back. I couldn't help it. "Hey, I got another question for you."

"Shoot."

"Sandy asked me if I wanted to go clubbing with her this weekend. What do you think?" I pushed the cart forward to the fruit and veggie section, my favorite part of the store!

"Um, I don't care if you go." Jacob's response was nonchalant.

"Would you want to come?" I asked.

"Not really. I don't like to dance."

"Oh, okay." My voice's sad echo rang in his eyes.

"Aww, what's wrong? If you want me to come, I will." He offered.

"Kind of. I wanted to drink, but I'm guessing the club Sandy wanted to go to will be downtown, and I'm not going to drive home like that." I reached for a few plastic bags.

"You drink?" He voice went up in tone.

"Not a lot. I was just thinking one or two, to celebrate." I smiled hollowly.

"Oh. Okay. Yeah, sure. I'll go." Jacob seemed to have calmed down. "Do I have to dance?" He whined.

"Absolutely!" I cracked up laughing.

"But I can't dance!" His whines continued. They were so cute!

"Well, you'd better learn!" I grinned.

"What are you doing tonight in a couple of hours?" Jacob asked, trying to change the subject.

"Probably watching a movie with Marie. Why? What's up?" I dropped a bag of fresh peaches in my cart.

"I didn't know if you wanted to hang out and talk after the game. I could stop by your place, if you wanted."

"Sure." I smiled, but my stomach wasn't setting comfortably.

"Rock on. I'll give you a call when it's done."

"Rock on. See you later." I smiled.

"Bye."

"Bye."

All of a sudden, I was inexplicably nervous. Was he rethinking this "taking it slow" thing? Was he not in the mood for a relationship? Maybe he'd decided I wasn't his type. Geez, I hoped not! There was something different about this guy, and I didn't want him to leave before I had the chance to figure out how he'd managed to cast such a captivating spell on me.

Chapter 24

"Baby girl, you need to relax. What is going on?" Alena's voice resonated concern.

"I don't know. He just said, 'I'll call you later'." I fretted. "In a relationship, isn't that like the kiss of death?"

"It can be, but it doesn't necessarily mean so. What else did he say?" She inquired.

"Well, he brought his mother to Happy Pets when he picked up the antibiotics." I began. "And he introduced me as his 'friend'."

"Oh, that's not good."

"No, it's not." I echoed.

"What else?" Her words were hollow.

"He keeps saying he wants to take things slow, but then he defines it as no sex. I didn't think that was slow." Thoughts and feelings swirled within my core, unable to stop their painful jabs from cutting my soul.

"Baby girl, I think you need to wait until you talk to him before you start to worry. For all you know, he could tell you something stupid and you're worrying for nothing." Alena lectured.

"Something stupid? Like what?" I furrowed my brows, trying to cut through the logical steps and jump to the end conclusion.

"Who knows? Maybe he's a virgin." She laughed.

"At 27?" I started laughing with her.

"Hey, stranger things have happened. You never know." She offered.

"True." I nodded slowly. I could feel my muscles melt into the couch cushions as Alena's goofy logic crossed through the air and came out the receiver of my cell phone.

"Besides, it's not like John hasn't said 'we need to talk' and it was over something stupid. Guys don't know how to properly communicate." She continued.

"What was it about?" I asked.

"When he wanted to pay the phone bill." Alena cracked up laughing again. " 'If the bill is due by the 15th of every month, I think we should pay it by the 5th at the latest.' What a dork!" Her sides sounded like they were splitting from the memory. "Get me all worried for nothing!"

"Wow! What a dork, indeed!" My worries floated away into outer space. That is, until my call waiting beeped.

"Oh honey. That's Jacob! Can I call you back?" I could feel my soul clam up, not wanting to face the prospect of this newfound relationship going south.

"Sure. Love you." She sang.

"Love you too." I quickly clicked over as soon as the words had left my mouth.

"Hey. What's up?" I tried to make the words come out sounding cool.

"Not much." Jacob replied.

"How was the game?" Not that I cared. I wasn't a big hockey fan.

"Not too bad. There weren't any fights, though." He sounded disappointed.

"Aw. I'm sorry about that." I stuck my lower lip out to show solidarity.

"It's okay. Maybe next time."

"Yeah." I began to nibble on my thumbnail, anxious to get this 'talk' over with.

"So, what's up with you?" Jacob's words were cool.

"Not much. Just talking to a coworker." I shrugged.

"Sandy?" Was it me, or did his voice cringe at her name?

"No, Alena." I corrected.

"Oh. Okay." He sounded thoughtful. "So, what are your plans for the rest of the night?"

"Nothing really. Why? What are your plans?" I threw the ball back in his court.

"Nothing. I didn't know if you wanted to get together and hang out."

"Sure. What would you like to do?" I asked. A knock at the door prompted me to wiggle free from the comfortable couch cushion.

"I don't know. What would you like to do?" Jacob smiled when I peeked open the door.

Tilting my head to the left with a smirk, I hung up the phone.

"That wasn't very nice." He laughed, walking through the door. I stuck my foot out behind him as I heard the bell on Marie Rose' collar get louder.

"Purr?" She asked.

"No, baby." I shook my head. She swished her tail at me.

"Hey." He smiled.

"Hey yourself." I raised my arms in a crescent moon shape, hoping he'd take the hint. Hook, line, and sinker! Jacob stepped towards me, wrapping his arms around my waist. I immediately jumped at the chance to intertwine my arms around his neck. He must've been around 6 feet tall, because I was able to nuzzle my face in my neck. Inhaling, I could smell his cologne, laundry detergent, and best of all, him. I closed my eyes, hoping to get lost in the moment.

"I missed you too." Jacob leaned his cheek against the top of my head.

"Mmm." I mumbled.

"So what would you like to do?" He took a small step back, looking in my eyes.

"What would you like to do?" I smirked.

"We could watch a movie, get something to eat… Anything you want."
He smirked back.

"I'm good with whatever." I brought my shoulder up to my ear.

"Are you hungry?" Jacob slowly brought his nose closer to mine until
they tickled each other. Scrunching my face, I smashed my right palm into
it and rubbed furiously.

"I guess. A little bit. Are you?" My voice came out nasally.

"I could go for dessert. I kind of ate a hot dog at the game." Jacob
blushed.

"Rock on. Where would you like to go?" Sadly, I ended the embrace to
retrieve my coat and my handbag.

"It doesn't matter to me." He shrugged.

"Okay. Well, if you want, we can drive around until we find something
that looks appealing." I offered.

"Sounds good to me." He smiled.

I smiled back. "Lead the way."

As we headed outdoors into the cold bitter winds, I waddled like a
penguin to keep my balance. Jacob sensed that footing was delicate, and

grasped a firm handle of my coat to steady me. As noble an idea as this

was, it unfortunately didn't pan out. Jacob lost his footing, and took me

down with him.

As we thudded to the ice covered pavement, I couldn't help but laugh.

"Oh my gosh! I'm so sorry! Are you okay?" His words were raw with

panic as fear gripped his eyes.

"I'm fine." My right hand flew to my derriere and began rubbing

furiously. "Nothing bruised but my ego." I smiled at him.

"Are you sure?" His concern was unwavering.

"I'm fine." I echoed, placing my left hand on the ground in an attempt

to stand up.

"How about you stay here while I go get the car?"

He offered.

"Okay." I nodded as I brushed of all remnants of my fall. My

peripheral vision told me he had marched off to the left in pursuit of his

vehicle.

I couldn't help but wonder if we were going to discuss "taking it slow".

And what did that even mean? Was it just no sex, or was everything else on hold as well? After all, he didn't introduce as his significant other to his mom.

Taking in the cold air, I waited impatiently for destiny to reveal herself to me.

Chapter 25

An older silver car slowed as it pulled up to the curb. Leaning forward, I could see Jacob in the driver's seat with a sheepish smile on his face.

"Hop in." Tilting to the right, Jacob unlocked the passenger side door.

"Nice ride." I teased, sliding into the seat.

"Hey, I can't complain. It's mine, it's paid for, and it runs great." He smiled at me.

"True. You've got a point there." I smiled back.

"So, where would you like to go?"

"I don't know how you feel about Chinese, but there's a good place around the corner." I pointed.

"Sure." Looking over his right shoulder, Jacob signaled to cross the dotted white line.

We rode listening to the hum of his engine, watching my hand gestures. My heart pounded with anticipation as the specific details of our relationship were dangled in front of me, cloaked in a translucent shroud of mystery.

As the car pulled into the parking lot, I clutched the seatbelt. It felt like my heart was on the fritz as every nerve threatened to misfire. As a result, none of my other extremities could function properly.

"What's wrong?" As Jacob's beautiful eyes fell on my shaking hands, my voice caught in my throat.

"NN. Cmm." I cleared my throat. "Nothing, why?"

"That's a lie. C'mon. Talk to me. Are you alright?" His warm soft hand encased mine.

"Just nerves. That's all." A fake smile waned across my lips.

"Nerves? About what?" Jacob wrinkled his soft blonde eyebrows and batted his blonde eyelashes.

"Well, at work, you said you were going to call me later, like you wanted to talk about something." I fidgeted with my zipper, my eyes on my knees.

"Oh, no." He laughed. "I just wanted to talk and hang out with you later."

"Really?" I looked up into his eyes.

"Yeah. Why? What were you thinking?"

"I don't know. I guess I thought you were rethinking this whole thing."
I shrugged.

"What would make you think that?" He tilted his head to the right.

"I don't know." I couldn't pinpoint the exact reason that thought
popped into my head.

"Don't be silly." His right hand slid over my hair, and his gentle lips
grazed my forehead. My heart did a back flip. "Come on. Let's get
something to eat."

"Are you sure you don't have any second thoughts?" I pushed.

"Yes, I'm sure." He unbuckled his seatbelt, and I followed suit. "Why
would I?"

"You said it yourself. You don't exactly have a type." My eyes opened
wide, as if to say, 'Ha! I got you there!'

"That's true. I don't." He nodded. "But I do know you're the only
person who's made me feel this way."

"What way?" I couldn't help but smirk as I watched him walk around
to my door.

"I don't know. I feel like I can tell you anything. It's weird. I hardly know you, but you're the only person I feel like I can be myself around." He smiled, offering his hand.

I grabbed the hand that he had extended, bracing myself as he pulled me into the frigid air. As we gazed into each other's eyes, I surrendered my reservations and took solace in his embrace.

Chapter 26

Exhaling my troubles away, I slurped my lo mein noodles while I watched Jacob dissect my fortune cookies.

"'Today, you will watch an awesome movie'." Jacob read.

"It doesn't say that!" I crinkled my nose at him, grabbing for the small rectangular paper. He just laughed.

"It says, 'Prepare to cash in on a smart investment'." I tossed it back at him.

"Oh, come on. The first one sounded better." Jacob grinned at me.

"You are such a dork." I rolled my eyes at him.

"Yeah, but you know you like it." He crinkled the bridge of his nose.

"Yeah, yeah." I pushed my lo mein to one side with a fork. Some people had the talent to eat Chinese with chop sticks. I was not one of them.

"Hey. I got a question for you." Jacob munched thoughtfully on the cookie.

"Shoot."

"How come you thought I was going to break up with you?" Leaning in, he placed his slightly rounded chin in his hands.

"I don't know." I paused for a second, trying to determine the origins of my worry. "I got a question for you."

"I'm listening."

"How come you introduced me to your mother as your 'friend'?" I looked him in the eyes, opening mine. I stared unblinking, waiting for an answer.

"I'm sorry. Did that upset you?" Jacob's eyebrows lowered.

"No, not really. I was just wondering." I lied, taking a bite.

"It's not that I don't want anyone to know. It's that my mom always disapproves of everyone I have anything to do with. She hates all of my friends, everyone I talk to, and especially anyone I bring home." He rolled his eyes, shaking his head from bad memories.

"I see. Is that what you meant by taking things slow?" My left cheek revealed a dimple's hiding place.

"Not really." Jacob's face turned a deep shade of maroon as he shielded my gaze with his jacket.

"Aww!! Are you blushing?" I squealed, pulling at his coat.

"No! Go away!" He pouted.

"That's so cute!" I laughed.

"Glad you think so." A single greenish eye peered out from behind the zipper. "I told you what it meant."

"Just no sex?" I reiterated.

"Yep. That's it." He remained hidden behind his polyester bodyguard.

"Any particular reason?" I sucked my cheeks in and wiggled my lips at him.

"Who's the dork?" Jacob erupted into laughter.

"I freely admit I'm a dork." I grinned with pride.

"Do you want to know the real reason why?" Jacob's eyes softened as his facial muscles relaxed.

"Sure." I shrugged. "No, wait! Do I?"

"You tell me."

"Yes."

"Okay. When I first saw you, I was drawn to your animal magnetism. Then, I brought Sera home and you gave me a crash course in small breed care, I couldn't get your smile and your sweet nature out of my mind. It has nothing to do with sex. I mean, don't get me wrong. Who wouldn't love to have sex? But that's not what I cherish about you. That's not what I miss when I'm not with you." Jacob reached across the table and placed his right hand on my left hand, offering a gentle squeeze.

"Aww!!!" I practically leapt across the table and threw my arms around him. My surprise attack caught him off guard, and we both nearly fell backwards. The people working gave us warning glares.

"Glad you think so." He smiled, our eyes centimeters away from each others. Navigating my torso around the edge of the table, I sat on his lap while maintaining our embrace.

"Absolutely!" I kissed his nose.

"You missed." He wiggled his nose up and down.

"Oh. My apologies." I kissed his cheek.

"Wow. Your aim is terrible!" He laughed.

"Considering there isn't a bull's eye on your face to tell me where I'm aiming…" I began, but Jacob's soft lips interrupted me, and I was glad to enjoy the silence.

I could feel his facial whiskers tickle around my mouth while the electricity flowed between us. My right hand instinctively caressed his right cheek, and his arms tightened their grasp around my waist.

Jacob pulled back a couple inches, and I stared speechless at him.

"What do you say we go watch a movie?" He smiled at me.

"Sure." I smiled back. "What movie would you like to watch?"

"Anything."

Chapter 27

Nothing could've been more perfect as we sat on my couch in front of the TV. I didn't even care what was playing. I was perfectly content with the company! I was oblivious to everything surrounding our perfect evening, including the time.

Jacob was sitting in the corner of the couch with the recliner up so he could stretch out his legs. I was sitting sideways, cuddled up against his torso with my legs sprawled along the rest of the couch. Of course, I was generous and relinquished control of the remote over to the house guest.

"What time is it?" Jacob looked around for a clock.

"I don't know. Press info on the remote." I pointed to the yellow button.

"Wow. It's 10:54pm! I can't believe it's that late already!" Shifting his weight, Jacob braced his arms by his hips in a successful attempt to stand up.

"Work?" I wrinkled my nose, saddened by his impending departure.

"Yeah." He didn't seem to happy about the fact that he had to leave anymore than I was.

"It's okay. We can always do something this weekend, if you don't have plans." Smiling, I tried to shine a ray of hope in this sea of departure.

"Is Saturday okay? I'm going to watch another hockey game on Friday with a couple of coworkers."

"Sounds like a plan. Have fun! Drive safe!" I wrapped my arms around his waist. In turn, his arms enveloped mine in a bear hug as his hand went soothingly up and down my back.

"You want to come?" He whispered in my ear.

"Where? To the hockey game?" My eyes darted back and forth, trying to spot his logic train.

"Sure."

"Not really. No offense, hockey isn't my favorite sport." I shrugged, his sweet chin lifted by my shoulder.

"Let me guess. Ice skating." He laughed.

"Ha ha. Very funny. Actually, believe it or not, I like football." I stated matter of factly, crinkling my nose at him.

"Oh really?" Who's your favorite team?" Jacob raised his right eyebrow.

"The AFC East Champions, of course." I grinned.

"Oh, geez." He shook his head.

"Why? Who's your favorite team?" I swished my nose across his.

"I don't really have one. I just like watching." Jacob shrugged.

"Maybe we could watch a game together." I offered, my eyes opened wide with hope at the prospect of cuddling once again on the couch. I've never known a football game to take less than 3 hours. 3 glorious hours curled up in his arms. Life couldn't have offered anything more precious!

"Maybe." Jacob smiled, his eyes softening.

"What?" I smiled back, sensing some thoughtful emotion just beyond my reach.

"It's nice to find someone I can cuddle with and watch sports."

My heart fluttered with happiness as his eyes continued to twinkle at me. Nuzzling my face in his neck, I took a deep breath and imprinted his pheromones onto my memory and savored the moment.

Chapter 28

"C'mon, girl! Spill! You've got to give me details!" Sandy begged, tugging on my smock.

"A lady doesn't kiss and tell." My chin grazed both shoulders.

"Who said you were a lady? C'mon! Just tell me!" She whined.

"You're not going to get anything." I laughed.

"You are so mean!" Sandy stormed off, leaving me to my papers.

"Why can't you give that kid a crumb, baby girl? It's not as if she found someone to settle down with." Alena's hands perched themselves on her hips, silently accusing me of mistreating my friends.

"She doesn't want a crumb. She's wants the whole loaf! Besides, there isn't much to tell."

"There's got to be something. How are things going?" She reached in between her legs and pulled an office chair to her, digging her heels into the floor for movement.

"Fine. We had dinner a couple of nights ago and watched TV. It was no big deal." I shrugged.

"Is he good to you?" Alena asked.

"Oh, he's wonderful." I smiled, my eyes sparkling at the fond memory of us falling together on the ice.

"Well, that's good." She smiled with me.

"It is." I nodded.

Chapter 29

"Mew?" Marie Rose asked, hopping onto the couch.

"Hi, honey. How's my little girl doing?" I cooed, reaching for her ear.
She ran away in terror, and I simply shrugged off her moodiness in favor
for channel surfing.

As I settled in with the remote in my hand, my thoughts drifted away to
a warmer place. I could see the images changing rapidly in front of my
eyes, but Jacob's unseen presence dominated my attention. I didn't know
what it was about him. He easily could've blended in with the rest of the
male population, and yet, he had stuck out from the very beginning.

Even though he was nowhere to be seen or heard from, my entire being
trembled as my heart fluttered away to greet the happy thoughts.
Everything about him captivated me. His smile, his eyes, the way he
laughed… everything.

Suddenly, the happy train was slammed with a ton of bricks. What if
Jacob decided that I wasn't his type? What if things didn't work out?
What if he wasn't really who he pretended to be? What if he was a

monster, like Michael? I tried my hardest to exhale all my worries, but they wouldn't break their hold on my psyche.

Desperately, I tried to shake free of the negative thoughts. Logically, I knew it was too early to tell what the future held for me and my beau. That didn't relieve me of any of my anxiety.

I tried to talk to the television set in a futile attempt to drive away the thoughts. "That looks good. I wonder if you can make it with avocados." "Seriously. Why would someone wear heels like that to a crime scene?" But nothing worked. So I reached for my cell phone in a foolish attempt to distract myself. I could hear the receiver begin to ring.

"Hello?" Sandy's bubbly voice sang.

"Hey lady. What's up?" I offered a hollow smile.

"Nothing. What's up with you?" She smiled back.

"Bored. Didn't know if you wanted to do something."

"Rock on! Do you want go to clubbing or drinking or what?" Sandy squealed with childlike delight.

"You pick." Deep down inside, I had the undeniable feeling that I shouldn't have opened this door, that this was a huge mistake. But I didn't care. I didn't want to be haunted by my thoughts.

"How about we meet at the Corner Spot?"

"Okay. Inside or outside?" I asked.

"Outside."

"Awesome. I'll see you in an hour." I stood up and headed towards my closet.

"Rock on! Later, babe!" Sandy sang.

Absently, I thumbed through my clothes. I didn't want to dress too cute (for fear of being hit on), but I didn't want to look like I just rolled out of bed either.

In the end, I had decided to go with a pair of hip hugger jeans, a fitted multicolored tee, and a pair of small heels. Nothing too sexy, nothing too ordinary.

I set out on foot towards the intersection of Main Street and Elm Drive, where I knew Sandy would be waiting. Tucking my head down, I breathed into my scarf to keep my face warm.

Why was I doing this? I wasn't a party animal. What would possess me to go out clubbing and drinking? Did I really think I could drive away my inner demons with alcohol?

Shaking my head, I kept on walking. Part of me wanted to turn around and go home, and just tell Sandy that I had changed my mind. Another part of me insisted that it was okay to indulge in wild behavior since I didn't do it that often.

Pushing all thoughts (logical or illogical) away from the forefront of my mind, I spotted Sandy's perky face beam with glee at my arrival.

"Woo-hoo! Let's do this!" She squealed, grabbing my jacket and dragging me into the club. Sandy was already wearing an id tag that told the bartender she was legal. Fetching my license, I displayed the picture to the inquiring bouncer who was kind enough to bestow the same bracelet.

Sandy and I immediately gravitated to the bar, exchanging cash and sobriety for alcohol and craziness. We danced, drank, and laughed the hours away. It wasn't until well into the night that I realized just how much the booze had begun to affect me.

All of a sudden, I was exhausted and dizzy. I was tempted to close my eyes and fall asleep right there on the dance floor. Instead, I watched Sandy popping up and down to the music. She was oblivious to my smaller tolerance.

"I'm going to get some air." I yelled over the noise. She nodded.

Slowly, I made my way through the rest of the people to the outside. The cold air shocked me back to my senses, but I was still too intoxicated to made heads or tails of anything. Deep down inside, I knew I had drunk enough to make myself vulnerable to any and everything in life.

Desperately, I wanted to go home and escape these feelings. Fear electrified my nervous system as I gripped my cell phone. I stood there shaking on the sidewalk as my phone sprang to life.

"Hello?" A groggy voice answered.

"Hey." I whispered.

"Hey, you. What's going on?" Jacob smiled.

"Not much. I was wondering if you could come pick me up." My voice was as soft and small as a child's.

"Sure. Where are you?"

"The Corner Spot. I'm right out front."

"What time is it?" He mumbled.

"I have no idea."

"Are you drunk dialing me?" He laughed.

"Maybe." I laughed. Was my inebriated state that obvious?

"Alright. I'm on my way. I'll be there in less than 10 minutes." He hung up the phone.

I began to bounce up and down as I looked around every street corner for Jacob's older silver car. I couldn't blame the cold or the alcohol. My inability to keep still stemmed from the magical hold he had over me.

"Hey, babe." A warm arm slid around my waist, causing me to jump.

"Geez! You scared the hell out of me!" I laughed.

"Sorry." He laughed with me. Lunging at him, I wrapped my arms around his neck and buried my face in his warmth.

"I missed you too. Would you like me to take you home?" His embrace was tender and firm.

"Yeah." I smiled.

"Come on, you lush." He shook his head.

"Hey now. It's not like I drink all the time." I raised a hand up in defense as we gingerly treaded towards his car.

"I certainly hope not!"

I didn't have a response. There was something in his voice that raised an internal alarm, but I was in no condition to be able to decipher the translation. I knew he didn't drink. Maybe he didn't because of an outstanding reason.

We drove back to my apartment in silence. I felt guilty and ashamed of my behavior. What was I thinking? Why did I allow the reckless part of me to take over?

I gave my best effort to assist Jacob in helping me up the stairs and into bed.

"Come on. Let's get some sleep." Pulling the covers up to my chin, I could feel his soft lips graze my forehead.

Dizzily, I closed my eyes. I could sense Jacob's body lying still next to me, his breathing steady and soothing. It was the most beautiful lullaby that I'd ever heard.

Before I knew it, I could feel the slight warmth of a stray sunbeam on my shoulder. My temples throbbed as I rolled away from the bright light, shuddering in the cold of the shadows. I tried to escape an impending hangover, but a deliciously foreign aroma seduced my nose. It was coming from an alien heat source.

My heart thudded against my ribcage as my subconscious told me that I wasn't alone. For a split second, panic and vulnerability seized my senses as I forced distance between me and this stranger.

"Everything okay?" Jacob's concerned voice shattered the silence. His angelic form lifted as he floated over towards me.

"Huh? Uh, yeah. I guess. What time is it?" I tried to find my way through the mental fog back to reality.

"Hold on. Let me check." His right hand fumbled around at his side. "8am."

Groaning, I stretched. The movement caused a hangover to crack down like Thor's hammer, rendering me immobile.

"You okay?" A hand lightly caressed my hair over and over, making my scalp tingle from affection.

"Been better." I smiled weakly.

"I believe it. You drink like that often?" He teased.

"No, not usually." I shrugged.

"Dare I ask what prompted last night?" His hand no longer lovingly stroked my hair, and I could feel my heart twinge with sadness.

"I don't know." I pulled the covers over my head, trying to block out the emotional thoughts and the physical effects that were trying to plague me.

"I got an idea. How about we get some more sleep, and I'll make you some soup when we get up."

I scooted closer to Jacob, nuzzling my nose into his chest as an answer.

Chapter 30

The second time consciousness greeted me, it was a little easier. My head ached slightly less, and the sunlight was a little more tolerable.

Opening my eyes, I could see Jacob's beautiful green babies staring back at me.

"You look so peaceful when you sleep." He smiled.

"You were watching me sleep?" I smirked at him. My heart melted a little.

"Yeah. I couldn't sleep any longer, so I decided to watch you."

"What time is it?" I stretched.

"Almost 11."

"Holy crap! I'm late for work!" Leaping out of bed, I ran over to my dresser.

"Hey hey hey. Relax. It's okay. I already talked to your boss. She called about an hour ago." His torso shot up in alarm, his left arm propping him up.

"What did she say?" My feet felt the icy chill of winter the bare floors had to offer as I stopped in my tracks.

"She wanted to know why you didn't come in. I told you were you out last night." he replied casually.

"And she said it was okay?" My voice sounded weak and tired.

"Yeah. She said you never take a sick day, and you're long overdue." Jacob patted the mattress. "Why don't you come lay down? You look pale."

"Hang on." I decided to make use of the lavatory before I looked in the mirror. He was right. My skin seemed ghoulishly white, almost wax like against my cheekbones.

Emerging from the small bathroom, I could see Jacob was right where I'd left him. Offering a faint smile, I climbed back into the warmth of the covers at his side.

"Thank you for coming to pick me up last night." I rolled over to face him.

"No problem. Any time you want a ride, let me know." He smiled. "May I ask what prompted last night?"

"I don't know." I sighed. I could feel a nagging sensation at the core of my soul, but I couldn't wrap my tongue around its sharp edges. I knew that Michael had burned me, leaving a sour taste in my mouth (as far as relationships went), and that I was scared this one was doomed to fail. Somewhere, on some level, I worried that it was my fault things didn't work out, and that I would ruin this wonderful chance at happiness lying next to me.

"Don't worry. I hardly go out like that, and I don't plan on doing it for a <u>long</u> while." I did my best to reassure him, even stroking his arm.

"I believe it. I just wanted to make sure everything was all right."

"Of course everything's all right. Why wouldn't it be?" I asked, puzzled.

"You don't strike me as an alcoholic." Jacob shrugged.

"I'm not! Why would you say something like that?" I crinkled my nose in confusion.

"It's been my experience that there are two kinds of people who drink in this world. One kind of person drinks to drink, and the other drinks to forget something, like pain or fear."

His words plucked at a heart string.

"Sorry. No, I'm not an alcoholic." I shook my head. "I guess that makes me the second kind of drinker."

"Aww. What's bothering you? Talk to me." It was his turn to start petting my arm. Scooting closer, I nuzzled happily into his warmth.

"Just nervous about dating, I guess." I wiggled my left shoulder around.

"How come?" He wrapped his arm around me.

"The last time, I didn't do so well."

"This time's different." He smiled.

"How so?" I gazed into his eyes, searching for an answer.

"Because this time, you've got me at your side."

Chapter 31

Tenderly, Jacob sat on the edge of the bed. He lowered himself slowly as he lifted the bowl in his hands up.

"Oh my gosh! You actually made me soup?" I laughed.

"I said I would." He grinned at me.

Waiting patiently, Jacob sat there contently while I sat up. Opening my hands, I offered to relieve him of his bowl holding duties. He gladly accepted the reprieve.

As I stared at his beautiful green eyes, I couldn't help but fall for Jacob a little bit more. The last person to make me soup in bed when I didn't feel well was my mother. Michael never cared enough about me or my health to perform such a nice gesture. I took a sip of broth.

"Is it too hot?" He leaned in.

"No. It's fine." I smiled. Honestly, it was a little tepid. But I wasn't going to complain.

"Are you sure Alena is okay with me taking today off?" I asked. I couldn't help but feel guilty for playing hooky.

"I'm sure. You're welcome to call and ask her yourself." He blinked.

"What about you?" The radical idea popped out of my mouth before I was aware of it consciously.

"What about my job?" Was it me, or was his response satirical?

"Yeah. You're not going to get in trouble for not going to work, are you?" I couldn't help but feel incredibly selfish and guilty for depriving Jacob of his normal daily rituals.

"I called in sick." He waved sideways. "Besides, I promised you I would take care of you." With a smile, Jacob stroked my leg.

"But I feel so bad." I whined, pouting at him.

"Well then, maybe you shouldn't drink like that." Jacob laughed, playfully elbowing me.

"Careful. You're going to spill the soup." I laughed.

"Then hurry up and eat it." He teased.

"I'm working on it." I took another sip. "I take it you don't drink."

"What would make you say that?" Jacob cautiously asked.

"It's just a guess, judging by your disapproval." I shrugged.

"No, I don't drink." He shook his head. I watched as the sun made his gentle blonde hair glitter like a diamond.

"Any particular reason why not?" Finishing the soup off with a loud slurp, I put the bowl down on the bed and wiped off the remaining liquid on my muzzle with the back of my wrist.

"My uncle is an alcoholic. He drinks 2 bottles of vodka a day. Honestly, I'm surprised he hasn't gotten in a car accident." I could see sadness resonating far away in his eyes, deep down in the bottom of his soul.

"Does he drive drunk?" I was flabbergasted by the possibility!

"Sometimes. I guess he's done it with me in the car when I was little. When my dad realized that, I wasn't allowed to spend time with him anymore." Jacob's voice was filled with sadness. It broke my heart to hear his pain.

"Oh. I'm sorry." My voice was quiet.

"Not your fault." His left arm rubbed my back, causing a shiver to run parallel along my spinal chord. At the same time, I adored and abhorred the effect he had on me. It was crazy!

"So what would you like to do?" With a hollow smile, I tried to lighten the mood.

"We could go back to sleep." He shrugged.

"We can't sleep the whole day away!!" I scoffed, nudging him with my shoulder.

"Not with that attitude!" He nudged me back, and we broke into laughter. "So what would you like to do?"

My eyes absorbed the radiating beauty from his face as I scanned my entire brain for an answer. I knew that if a decision being made depended on me, I could probably produce. The problem was my head and my heart were having difficulties communicating. My head took the logical approach to recovering from a night of reckless behavior, but my heart didn't care what occurred. As long as Jacob was by my side, I was content.

Chapter 32

With the volume down low, we attempted to watch a movie. Unfortunately, I was too preoccupied with watching Jacob to watch the movie!

He was so different than Michael, in almost every way. Superficially, they had their similarities. But what struck me the most was the subtle differences. For example, Michael never watched movies with me. He couldn't be bothered to sit still long enough to cuddle with me. As a result, I was on edge most of the time I was around him. Jacob, on the other hand, seemed perfectly content just sitting back and observing life. It was so easy to relax around him. It was such a peaceful feeling to know that I could let my guard down, that I didn't have to be on edge or always on the go, and that in some physical or mental capacity I had to be active. I could just relax.

Jacob saw me smiling at him. It must've inspired him to reach over and pet my matted hair. Even though his touch was light, my head screamed in agony.

"I'm so sorry! Are you okay?" His face contorted in fear as I winced.

"Yes. My head still hurts a bit." I peeked through a mostly closed left eye.

"Would you like a cup of tea?" Jacob pushed himself off the bed, almost as if he'd made up his mind before I answered.

"Sure, I guess." I smiled weakly at him.

"Anything for you, babe." He smiled back, then disappeared into the kitchen.

"Right back at you." My heart did a somersault.

Chapter 33

"It's weird. Things with Jacob are so different than they were with Michael." My vision blurred as my eyes took in all the sights around me, my mind desperately trying to pin down my feelings.

"How so?" Alena's brows furrowed in confusion.

"I don't know. It's hard to explain." I mimicked her facial expression.

"Maybe we could go out for drinks later and talk about it, if you want." Alena teased.

"Sure, okay." I groaned, my head still reeling from last night.

"Serves you right. You should've listened to your gut instinct and not partied with Sandy." Alena lectured.

"Yes mother. Sorry mother." I rolled my eyes. A sharp pain shot through my head from my ocular sockets, causing me to moan.

"Are you okay?" Jacob called from the kitchen.

"I'll live." I called back.

"Is he there with you now?" Alena's voice rose in excitement.

"Yes. He gave me a ride home last night." I replied softly. Even though it was my own voice, the sound caused my temples to throb.

"Did he sleep over?"

"Yes."

"In the same bed?" She sounded like she was on the edge of her seat.

"Yes, but don't get the wrong idea. He slept on top of the covers." I corrected.

"Why would he do that?" The pieces didn't add up for Alena. However, I was the wrong person to ask for clarification.

"How should I know?" I shrugged.

"Well, that was very sweet of him to pick you up." She smiled.

"Yes, he's a sweetie." I smiled back.

"It was so cute when I called your phone earlier and he answered!" She squealed. "He said you weren't coming in today because you were drinking last night, and that he was going to make you chicken soup when you woke up."

"Aww. Isn't he so sweet?" My heart soared.

"Absolutely. Consider yourself lucky baby girl. They don't make guys like that very often."

"Don't I know it?" I agreed.

Cautiously, Jacob entered the room with a slightly steaming cup of tea.

"Hey babe. I've got to go. I'll see you tomorrow at work, okay?"

"Call me first. I want to know you're feeling better." Alena said.

"Okay. I love you."

"Love you too, baby girl." I hung up the phone.

"Here's your tea." Jacob eyes smiled at me. I love the way his eyes crinkled!

"I was just talking to Alena." Looking up into those beautiful eyes, my heart ached at the guilt of telling another person I loved them. Logically, I knew it was silly. That was one of the 'lessons' I had 'learned' from Michael. His abusive ways knew no boundaries.

"Hey, it's okay. I know how girls are towards each other." Jacob shrugged it off.

I sat there, my mouth flapping wide open in disbelief. He wasn't upset that I had said I love you to someone else. He wasn't jealous. In fact, it didn't seem to faze him one bit!

As we cuddled up to each other in the comforts of the blankets, countless thoughts and emotions transcended the silence between us. Not a word was spoken.

Chapter 34

Lying there in the dark, my heart ached. Jacob had left a few hours prior to do laundry, leaving me alone with only my thoughts and Marie to keep me company. I was lonely. When I was with Jacob, the rest of the world disappeared, taking its misery and selfishness and destruction with it. I had no choice but to face the angst Destiny had to offer when I was alone.

I reached towards a temporarily distraction. Marie began to purr softly, tilting her head as I scratched behind her ears. For a split second, my soul delighted in the rays of happiness that beamed off of her whiskers. But the heartache pushed past the obstacle, rearing its ugliness right in my face. Even memories of Jacob didn't deter the monster.

And what are you going to do when this relationship ends? You know it's too good to be true. Why would something this wonderful stay in your life? Fairy tale endings may happen, but not to you.

I cringed at the harshness of the words whispered deep into my subconscious. I knew only time would reveal the future. But what if it was as bleak as my darkest fears made it out to be?

You tried so hard to make things work with Michael, and look how that ended. Don't lie to yourself. You know damn well that it doesn't matter what you do. Things with Jacob won't last.

I could feel the icy chill of fear's blade slide in between my ribs, causing my heartbeat to thrash in protest. The temperature in the room dropped significantly as the nightlife carried on. I was a prisoner, unable to escape from the hellish torture of the "What if?" monster.

Marie was oblivious to it all, relishing in her feline delight. Who knew that so much joy could be obtained by so little?

Chapter 35

I felt the sting of the cold air in my lungs. It was still dark outside, so I knew it had to be in the wee hours of the morning. The streets outside had long since ceased to provide the masses with entertainment, and Marie had made herself comfortable underneath the covers. Her breathing was shallow and even as she threw her small breath against my calf.

Oh, to be a cat. My thoughts echoed in the solitude. *I wonder what it would be like to have a worry-free existence.*

Glancing at the clock, I could see it read 5:02am. I felt mentally awake, yet physically drained. *Might as well get the day started, but not without my coffee!*

Without an inkling of any communication along the neural highway, I ripped back the covers to hop out of bed. The second my skin came in contact with the icy fingers of winter, every single hair follicle simultaneously did the wave as my body shook against the cold. My feet cringed upon contact with their slippers that patiently waited all night on the floor and my hands blindly roamed the cotton tundra in search of a bathrobe.

Wading through the air, I navigated to the kitchen. I knew this apartment forwards and backwards, dark or light, cold or hot. I knew where everything was placed within an inch of every boundary.

Rubbing my hands together near the coffee pot was a futile attempt at stealing warmth. I could hear the percolating of the beans and the dripping of my liquid breakfast as my mouth salivated from the delectable aroma. The scent of the dark roast bean wafting in the air was reminiscent of a security blanket, the way it warmed you from the inside out as it treated your esophagus like a water chute, and for a brief moment in time, you could close your eyes and disappear completely in a sip of this dark and delicious liquid.

I leaned against the kitchen counter as tangible thoughts danced in the air. I could see ideas swirling around in the steam, trying to formulate into tangible execrations. There they were, taunting me. The idea that Jacob and I weren't going to last. Right there! Rising up in the mist of the coffee! And there's another idea! That somehow, Michael and I not working out was my fault, though I had no idea how. The wicked idea

scolded me for contributing to the demise of a four year investment, and I

objurgated it. *I don't think so! I tried my damnedest to make things work!*

It's not my fault Michael chose drugs over me! I glared at the dust

particles, ire radiating in my pupils.

I shook my head violently, trying to bat the negative air around me

away with my hair. Concentrating on my breathing, I tried to blow my

remaining troubles away. There was only one way I was going to quash

these pesky anxieties. I was going to have to place a phone call to the most

omnipotent being I knew.

Chapter 36

I waited impatiently as the phone rang in my ear. I heard her angelic voice sing in my ear as the ringing stopped.

"Hello?" She asked. I smiled at her question. Just the sound of her innocence warmed my heart.

"Hey mom."

"Hey sweetie! What's going on?" She returned my smile.

"Not much. I just realized I haven't talked to you in a while, and I thought I'd catch up with you." Glancing out the window, I could see the sun making a glorious appearance as it painted the horizon with an array of iridescent hues. Lucky for me, my mother had always been an early bird.

"Well, isn't that so thoughtful of you! I was talking to your father yesterday about putting a garden in the backyard. Then we could have fresh veggies! Isn't that delightful?" Mom chirped.

My stomach growled at the thought. "Actually, it does mom." I could see her standing before me, slicing a zucchini lengthwise and stuffing it with ricotta cheese and covering with marinara sauce. I could always count on my mother to tantalize my senses with wholesome ingredients. Just talking about the possibilities caused my heart to glow with remembrance.

"So, what's new with you? Are you still working at that animal place?" Mom asked.

"Yes I am. I love working with animals, Mom. You know that!" I shook my head and smiled. "Actually, that's why I called. I do have some new news."

"Oooo! Do tell! C'mon, missy! Spill it! Is it a boy?" Mom squealed. I could hear rustling from her end of the phone.

"What are you doing?" I laughed at the commotion.

"I'm just clearing a spot at the table so I can sit down." I could just imagine her small bony hands furiously moving back and forth, her brown curls that had been flavored with time precisely put in place by a woman with prestige, honor, and 50+ years to practice her craft. "Okay, I'm listening. Give me all the details!"

"You are just like a school girl!" I laughed. "Possibly worse!"

"I may be older than you but I'm not dead. I can enjoy a good piece of gossip every once in a while. Now, start talking! I want to know all about it!" Mom retorted.

"Okay, well his name is Jacob, and he's a computer technician. He has a miniature Pomeranian named Sera who's sick. That's how we met. He brought her into my work so she could receive treatment." A smile graced my cheeks, causing them to blush with happiness at the memory.

"You met someone? How old is he?" Mom asked.

"27." I replied.

"That's nice. Not too much older than you. So when are you going to introduce him to the family?"

"Mom!" I scowled. "We've only been dating a couple of months! Can you wait a little bit before you start harassing him?"

"I'm not harassing him. I just want to make sure he's good enough for my baby. I can't help being protective." She cooed.

"I can take care of myself, mom." I rolled my eyes.

"I'm not saying you can't. I'm just saying that Michael was a wolf in sheep's clothing, and I want to make sure this guy isn't as well."

"His name is Jacob." I corrected.

"Fine. Jacob. Whatever. So when do I get to meet him?" She reiterated. I loved her sass. My mother was the kind of women you did not show weakness in front of. She could get to the true intentions of any soul with a single stare down. That would explain why my father was always so quiet!

"I don't know. I could text him and see when he's available if you'd like." Shrugging, I tried to be helpful.

"Do that."

What are you doing later?

I don't know yet, why?

My mom wants to meet you. Eek!

Hahaha. I get out of work at 6. How about after that?

Sounds good. Where do you want to meet?

Anywhere. You pick.

How about that little Italian place near my work?

Sounds good. What time?

How about right after work?

Sounds like a plan.

"Okay mom. We're going to meet him at an Italian restaurant near his work around 6pm. Does that work for you?" I relayed the conversation.

"Is that what all that clicking was about?" She laughed.

"Yes mother. But you got your answer." I smiled.

"Are you going to escort an old lady, or am I going to meet you there?"

"Be ready at 5pm, mom. I'll pick you up."

Chapter 37

Mom and I sat comfortably at a back table picking at a complementary basket of garlic bread. She nibbled contently as we sat in silence. The restaurant was dimly lit by lamps desperately trying to pass themselves off as candles. The table cloths were white with faint stains of spaghetti sauce from dinners served many, many meals ago. The silverware had been set delicately in place next to a porcelain plate, both of which had seen better days. The dust particles stared accusingly at me as they danced around my head. I glared at them, wanting nothing more than to strangle each individual one.

"What's that face for?" Mom started laughing at me.

"What face?" I could feel my forehead muscles soften.

"You're scowling at air!" She managed to sputter out her words as she kept her sides from splitting apart.

"Sorry mom. I just have a lot on my mind." I shook my head, trying to clear away the cobwebs.

"Well, talk to me baby. I'm your mother. If there's anything I can do to help, let me know. That's what I'm here for." Smiling, she rubbed my hand. I knew she sensed what was going on. Neither one of us could come up with the appropriate words to describe what was going on inside of my head, but we knew it was there.

"I don't know." I sighed.

"Is it work related?" She furrowed her brows.

"No. Work's fine. Everything great." I smiled hollowly.

"Is it Jacob? Is there something going on that I show know about?" Concern resonated in her vocal chords.

"No mom. He's wonderful. Trust me, you'll absolutely adore him." I smiled at his warm memory. I couldn't help it.

"Leslie, you're being vague. Is something bothering you or not?" Mom lectured.

"Sorry mom. I'm not trying to be. Yes, something's bothering me, but I'm not quite sure how to explain it." I fumbled with my words. Translating emotions into words could be difficult at times.

"Just do you're best. If it doesn't come out right the first time, then try again." Mom rubbed my hand some more.

"Okay, I'll try." Taking in a deep breath, I closed my eyes. "I guess I'm worried about Jacob."

"I thought you said he was wonderful." She tilted her head at me, trying to see my logic.

"He is. At least, I think he is. I don't know. I'm confused." I exhaled.

"Leslie…" Mom stared sternly.

"What if he's not that good of a guy?" I blurted, immediately retracting my lower lip and using it as a chew toy.

"Well, either he is or he isn't. Which is it?"

"I think he is. But then again, I thought Michael was." I frowned.

"Is that what this is about? Oh honey…" Mom's shoulders dropped, and the tension visibly floated off of her temples. "Jacob isn't Michael. You can't compare the two. I know that you and Michael were together for a long time, but he was a loser. He knew exactly what to say or do to make you stick around. I told you I didn't like him from day one."

"Alena said he was emotionally abusive." My voice came out quiet. My heart began thumping wildly, causing my entire body to shake. I knew my mother wouldn't lie to me, but did I want to hear the truth?

"Yes he was. That's one of the reasons I never let you bring him over to my house." Mom nodded, agreeing with Alena.

"What if Jacob turns out to be a loser too?" I fretted.

"Then I'll tell you, and you can get rid of him, and that'll be the end of that." She smiled reassuringly.

I offered a half hearted smile. I couldn't put any enthusiasm in a lie.

"You don't think there's something wrong with you, do you?" Mom raised a brow at me.

I shrugged. "What if there is? What if I'm somehow causing this?"

"Leslie! That is the most ridiculous thing I've ever heard come out of your mouth! Stop right there! What the hell could you possibly have done to deserve being treated like that? And it's not like you made Michael behave that way. That's who he is. That doesn't make you a bad person!" Mom snorted, trying to blow the nonsense away with a fierce breath.

"Sorry mom. I can't help but worry." I shrugged.

"I know, baby. But let's worry about the future when it becomes the present, okay? Now, where is this new beau of yours?" Mom popped her head up and looked around. She reminded me of a prairie dog.

Glancing at the clock on the wall, I caught Jacob looking around out of the corner of my eye. Smiling, I waved him over. My inner child did a somersault inside of me as he walked over to us. I felt like a princess in a far away land who had just spotted her savior from the loneliness of the dank tower that had imprisoned her. I could see a beautiful bouquet in his arms, and I couldn't help but feel spoiled. I stood up to accept an embrace.

"Hi honey." I smiled, wrapping my arms around his neck.

"Sorry I'm late. Work was hectic. You know how it goes." Jacob wrapped an arm around my waist and leaned towards my mother. "These are for you." He extended the flora towards her.

"Why thank you! That's very thoughtful of you." Mom smiled, accepting the flowers.

I blushed a little, feeling foolish for thinking the gift was for me. It didn't even occur to me that they might've been for someone else!

"Mom, this is Jacob. Jacob, this is my mother." I waved introductions. They reached towards each other, shaking hands vigorously. I couldn't help but feel guilty for getting jealous of my mother. They were flowers, after all. It's not like it was a marriage proposal!

"Have you ladies ordered yet?" Jacob smiled at me. He gently placed his jacket over the back of his chair, and scooted closer to me as he sat down.

"Not yet. We were waiting for you." I smiled as he gingerly touched the back of my hand. Every nerve tingled with delight as the sensation of love traveled up my arm and into my soul.

"What do you recommend?" Mom asked, peering at the menu. Her glasses were pushed down to the point of her nose and her mouth was slightly ajar with an inquisitive nature as she examined the list.

"I personally can vouch that the fettuccini alfredo is divine." Jacob's voice was strange, as if it were a puppet master speaking for him. He flashed his entire set of pearly whites at my mother. I groaned inwardly, rolling my eyes. There was nothing more embarrassing than being with a pretentious person. I wanted to crawl under the table and leap into an imaginary vortex that would teleport me to anywhere but in the midst of this situation!

"Does it come with broccoli and chicken?" Mom asked.

"I don't know. You can ask them." Jacob smiled again. I shot him a dagger look. His eyebrows furrowed in confusion. I shook my head.

"Would you excuse us, mother?" Standing up from the table, I jerked my head towards the entry way at Jacob. Silently, he stood up with me.

"Do you want me to order for you, or do you want me to wait?" Mom's face wrinkled with confusion.

"Just get me what you're having." I smiled.

"And for you, young man?" Mom peered at Jacob.

"What the heck. Why not make it three orders?" Jacob and mom shared a light hearted laugh.

"Three orders it is, then."

With a speed that would make Hermes jealous, I pinched the edge of Jacob's shirt and dragged him into the front entry way of the restaurant.

"What are you doing?" I hissed, my eyes bulging out in disbelief.

"What?" Jacob stared back, clueless to his treacherous shenanigans.

"You're being fake!" I accused, shaking my head.

"I'm sorry. It's not like I've done this before." He shrugged.

"Done what?" I pried.

"This is my first serious relationship. I don't know how I'm supposed to act." Jacob's lower lip pouted. It was so cute! "What if your mother doesn't like me?"

"Why wouldn't she like you?" I asked.

"I don't know." He shrugged again.

"Well, I can tell you that you stand a much better chance with her if you're honest. Don't be someone you're not. Just be yourself." I began to lovingly stroke his right arm. The maitre d caught the gesture out of the corner of his eye and raised a conspicuous eyebrow at us. My intuition said he didn't approve of my public display of affection.

Jacob exhaled loudly.

"It matters to me that she like you, but in the end, it's my decision on whether or not I want to keep seeing you." I smirked at him.

"I know. I'm sorry. I'll be myself from now on. I promise." He kissed my forehead.

"That's all I ask. Just show her the real you, the you that I adore." I grinned.

"Sounds like a great idea. How about we go join her now?" Jacob kissed my forehead, and jutted his elbow out. With a smile, I slid my arm around his and we walked back to the table. I could feel everyone's eyes on us, and I couldn't have cared less. I felt like the luckiest person on the planet!

"Is everything okay?" Mom asked. Her eyebrows were slightly ruffled with concern.

"Yes ma'am. I couldn't find the present I got for Leslie. I thought maybe I had dropped it, but I found it. It was in a different pocket." Jacob's entire demeanor has returned to normal. I couldn't help but smile as the real Jacob began to shine.

"Well, isn't that sweet of you?" Mom smiled.

"That's Jacob for you." I smiled at mom.

"So where is it?" Mom's eyes widened with suspicion. She was no fool.

I bit my lower lip, afraid of the impending humiliation in the moments to come. There was nothing I could say or do to change what was about to happen.

"They're right here." The jacket that Jacob had draped over his chair swallowed his entire hand as he valiantly went into his pocket to retrieve the trinkets that his attire had confiscated.

They were rectangular in shape; white with black markings. They were smaller than the size of a dollar bill, and my mouth twisted in bewilderment. Jacob propelled the paper presents over to me with his beautiful hand.

"What are they?" Mom beat me to the punch.

"I bought two front row tickets to the AFC East champions. I thought I would take Leslie to one of their home games. They're blank, so we can see whatever game you want this season." Jacob's eyes softened as his fondness for me that radiated from his irises blew mine kisses.

"Aww. Well isn't that sweet? Leslie, what do you say?"

For a moment, I was speechless. I couldn't believe that Jacob had gone to such extraordinary lengths to make me happy. My eyes swam around in mists of joy as I fumbled with my tongue.

"You didn't have to do that." My hand reached over to his in search of warmth, comfort and shelter. Our waitress appeared in stealth mode. Knowing that a tender moment was happening, she silently placed our food in front of us. I could sense a heartwarming smile upon her lips.

"I know I didn't have to, but I wanted to. I just want to make you happy." Jacob's words wrapped my soul in the most soothing and encompassing blanket of love I'd ever experienced. Out of the corner of my eye, I could see mom's overprotective instincts begin to ease.

Chapter 38

"You're a very lucky person. Jacob really cares about you." Mom

daydreamed into the rays of moonlight that brightened up her quaint tile

kitchen. Under normal light, the black tiles glittered with pride. But the

midnight rays eerily danced across the floor.

"I know mom, but what do you think of him?" I pressed.

"I think he's a good guy who really cares about you and you're

incredibly lucky to have him. So you'd better be good to him! And don't

let this one slip through your fingers!" She laughed.

"Wasn't planning on it, mom." I laughed with her.

"Good. Is he the 'One'?" Her question caught me off guard.

"What?" I couldn't wrap my mind around what she was asking.

"Do you think he's your soul mate?" Mom rephrased her curiosity. Her

eyes gazed into mine as she searched for an answer. Good luck finding it!

I didn't have that kind of knowledge!

"I don't know. It's entirely possible." I shrugged, unsure of the future

between me and Jacob. Who knows what could happen in 50 years?

"Do you want him to be?"

"Of course I do! He's absolutely wonderful! I'm not stupid, mom." Her goofy question made me snort.

"I'm sorry. I wasn't calling you stupid. I just know that a lot of you kids nowadays get divorced and throw the towel in too soon, rather than sticking around when things get tough." Mom glided on a cloud of contentment over to me and refilled my hot water mug. I yo-yoed the tea bag, coaxing the delicious flavor out of its sealed confinement.

"You need to remember that any relationship you have won't be perfect." Mom passed on a tidbit of wisdom.

"Mom! I'm not going to bounce from guy to guy!" I whined at her insinuation.

"No honey. That's not what I meant. Even if the relationship is platonic, there will be rough patches. You need to learn forgiveness, when to compromise, and when to stand your ground." Mom slid into her chair and began to mimic my hand motions.

"Oh. I know mom." I smiled at the clarity.

"He's a really good guy." Mom smiled.

"I know mom." I smiled with her.

"You're really lucky to have someone who cares so much about you."

"I know mom." My heart beamed with joy and pride at having snagged one of the elusive "good guys" on this planet. The dust particles pranced in the shadows, their rotten existence all but a distant memory.

"You have my approval."

Chapter 39

I happily hummed pop tunes that the radio had been blasting at me all morning as I strutted around the office. I had managed to find an angel walking around on earth, and he was all mine!

I bounced around the office with folders in my hand, relishing in the possibilities that the future teased me with. Was Jacob the one for me? Would we be getting married? What kind of a wedding would it be? What kind of a life would we spend together? Did Jacob want to have children? Would things always be so wonderful? I couldn't help but tantalize my brain with the endless opportunities.

Just wait until the girls get here! *I can't wait to tell them how dinner with my mother went*!

I hadn't noticed the bell sounding as someone walked into the office. I was way up in the clouds dancing when a familiar voice shot me down with a bullet of loathing despair.

"Hi Leslie. Long time, no see." His voice was icy cool, causing my skin to immediately ripple. My memory thrashed against the past, desperately straining to remember.

I turned around, not sure of the moments to come. But when I saw his face, everything came rushing back to me. Ire blurred my vision. My hands went rigid, curling into themselves. My whole body froze. I couldn't breathe. I couldn't move. I couldn't blink. The only sounds that were distinct were the radio blasting and the file folders clashing against the floor.

"What the hell do you want?" I hissed, glaring into his cocky face.

"My sister's cat is sick, so I brought her in. This is a vet's office, isn't it?" He grinned sadistically at me. He knew his presence caused me immeasurable angst.

"We're not the only veterinary office in town, Michael. You can take your sister's cat to a different facility." My tongue forced my words through clenched teeth.

"But I'm already here, so why should I take Snuggles to a different place?" His cocky arrogance managed to find my last nerve first.

I just stared in silence. I wasn't about to back down. I was tired of his games. That why I had ended our long term relationship. And he wouldn't leave me alone. Michael could not let go of his controlling games. It didn't matter if he made me miserable. As long as he was controlling the situation and manipulating my emotions, Michael was content.

I heard the bell open, and the girls stopped when they entered the show down. Sandy hid behind Alena, and they just froze in observation.

"Good afternoon, ladies. I was just explaining to Leslie that my sister's cat is sick and needs to be seen by a vet." Michael smiled pretentiously at Alena. She stood her ground, and simply folded her arms across her chest. Sandy scampered off to the back without uttering a word.

"And as I explained to Michael, there are other veterinary offices in town. He doesn't need to come here." I hissed.

"But what about Snuggles? She's really sick." Michael pouted.

"Then where is she?" Alena asked coolly.

"Excuse me?" Michael blinked, his perfectly pompous composure faltering for a split second.

"If Snuggles is so sick, then where is she?" Alena looked around for a cat carrier. I just smiled at her wise observation.

"I left her in the car." Michael's voice came out softly.

"Then I suggest you go keep her company while you escort her to another facility. Goodbye, Michael." Alena turned on her heels and headed towards Sandy's escape route.

"You heard the boss. Goodbye, Michael." I sneered, an evil grin spreading across my lips.

I heard the bell again. My heart sank. An actual customer! What were we going to do?! My mind frantically raced for a solution. We were called 'Happy Pets' not only because we loved animals, but because we tried to create a happy environment! Michael was going to ruin our reputation!

"Uh, hi. I'm here for the surgery." Jacob cautiously entered the battlefield with Sera squirming in his arms.

I wanted nothing more than to cover Jacob's beautiful loving eyes while I stabbed Michael furiously until the arrogance faded from his hateful deceiving eyes. I wanted to watch the light disappear, along with all of my troubles.

"Come on, dear. I'll get you set up." Alena busted into the front lobby from behind the receptionist's desk.

"Is everything okay?" Jacob's eyebrows wrinkled in confusion. He'd never seen me put in this emotional state before, and he was obviously concerned.

"Peachy." My voice was icy cold, and my heart twinged with guilt at my cruel response.

"Come on, sugar." Alena tugged at his shirt. "Let's take care of the little one."

I could see fear in Sandy's eyes as she peered at us from around the corner. My heart broke as Jacob walked away, and I wanted to fling myself into his arms, into his protective circle, where Michael could never reach me.

A wickedly vindictive smile crossed my face as flashing lights came to a stop in the parking lot. A large man with his fingers in his belt walked through the door.

"Is there a problem?" Sergeant Saroka asked.

"He needs to leave." I pointed at Michael.

"I told you. My sister's cat is sick. Why won't you help Snuggles?" Michael protested.

"Michael, you were told never to harass me again! That's what the police told you the last time you tried to break into my house! Now leave!" I screeched.

"This is a public place! Or did you forget that?" Michael yelled.

"That may be so, but there are other vet's offices you can go to. You don't need to be here! You were told to stay a minimum of 50 feet away of me at all times!" I yelled back.

"Says who?" Michael challenged.

"Says the order of protection I filed with the county!" I darted my head to the left in a "ha!" moment.

When Jacob heard me yell my ex's name, he came storming out from behind the desk and wrapped a territorial arm around my waist. "Why didn't you tell me that's what was going on?" He whispered in my ear.

My gaze didn't waiver. I could trust Michael to steal a yard if I took my eyes off of him for one second.

"Is that true, young man?" The cop asked.

"But my sister's cat…" Michael protested.

"Then where is the cat carrier?" I repeated Alena's question.

"I told you. It's in the car." He reiterated.

"Young man, is there an order of protection in place?" Sergeant Saroka was quickly losing patience with Michael's manipulative games.

"I don't know." He lied. Michael knew darn well there was! His face sank, as if he suspected that he wasn't going to win this fight.

"Yes there is. If you'd like, I can get the copy I have in my purse. It's right over there." I pointed to behind the desk.

"Please do that." The officer smiled weakly at me. I got the feeling that this wasn't his favorite part of the job.

As proud as a peacock, I waived a yellow piece of paper in Michael's face. "Signed by a judge." I gladly handed over Exhibit A to the tolerant man sworn to maintain peace in even the most chaotic of situations.

"So I see. Would you like to press charges?" He asked me.

"Yes I would." I smiled.

"Young man, please put your hands behind your back." The cop removed the handcuffs from his belt.

I was unable to interpret the frantic screaming that spewed forth from Michael's mouth. As soon as he realized he was going back to jail, he bolted through the door. That's when he began throwing curse words over his shoulders at me. The cop took off in pursuit, yelling into the radio attached to his collar bone.

"Are you okay?" Jacob's arms encircled me, and I melted into one giant shaking nerve. I buried my face in his chest and began mumbling obscenities.

"Honey, why didn't you tell me that's who it was?" His loving hands began stroking the back of my head.

"I'm sorry. I didn't want to involve you in this. All Michael does is start drama. He always has to control the situation and make it miserable for everyone." My eyes stung with an angry flow of tears, threatening to erupt.

"I take it he's the ex that didn't end so well?" Jacob asked innocently.

"That's putting it mildly." I rolled my eyes.

"Is there anything I can do?"

"Just hold me." I closed my eyes and breathed in Jacob's love.

I could hear the door open yet again. Looking up, I could see that Sergeant Saroka had returned.

"I'm going to have to put an APB on him. If he ever harasses you at home or at work, please call us. Every cop will be looking for him. Would you like a plain clothes officer to patrol your house?" His eyes resonated fear stemming from deep within his soul. Judging by my cousin's description, this was the same cop who had come to her rescue as a child. It appeared that Sergeant Saroka had seen his share of troubled times over the years as stress had permanently imbedded itself into lines around his face.

"I would like that." Jacob spoke up.

"Maybe. I don't know." I ran my hand over my forehead and onto my hair.

"It's your call." The cop offered.

"Is there a warrant out for his arrest?" I asked.

"Yes there is. As soon as anyone spots him, he'll be brought up on several charges." As the policeman removed his notepad from his belt, I saw blood dripping profusely from an unknown source.

"You're hurt!" I gasped.

"Michael was his name?" The cop asked. I nodded. "He had a knife on him. I had managed to tackle him to the ground. That's when he swung it at me and nicked my hand."

"Alena!" I shrieked. "Come quick!"

At hearing my panic, her blonde head emerged.

"What's wrong, baby girl?" She rushed over to me and Jacob.

"Michael stabbed the cop! We need to get him medical treatment!" I pointed at the bloody hand.

"It's okay. I've already radioed the station. They're sending backup and a bus." The cop dismissed my concerns with his good hand.

"That's fine, but for the time being, we can make the bleeding stop." Alena fetched a few adhesive bandages and reached for the cop's injury. Silently, she worked to stem the blood flow.

"Would you be willing to come down to the station, make a statement and file charges?" He asked.

"Certainly." I said.

"Sure." Jacob said in unison. I smiled up at him. He kissed my forehead.

"I'll be back in a bit, okay?" I asked Alena.

"Baby girl, you can take the rest of the day off as far as I'm concerned. Just call me later and let me know what happened. I want to make sure you're alright." Alena smiled at me.

"Are you coming?" I asked Jacob.

"What about Sera?" His heart pondered aloud.

"Don't worry about her. I'll take care of her. When Leslie calls me from home, I'll bring the pooch by. How does that sound?" Alena smiled with her hands on her hips.

"Who said I was going to be at Leslie's house?" Jacob grinned.

"With Michael running around on the loose?" Alena challenged.

"I think it's best if Leslie stayed at my house." Jacob pulled me over towards him, wrapping his massively muscular arms around my fragile waist.

"I agree. If he knows where you live, then you should only go home long enough to get a few necessities. You do have other places to stay that can keep you safe." The cop nodded.

I sighed, giving up the fight.

"Let me write down my address for you so you know where to bring Sera." Jacob hurried over to the front desk.

"We have it on file, honey. Go on. Everything will be taken care of." Alena shooed us out the door.

As I looked over my shoulder, I desperately wanted to go back to an hour before all the chaos had unfurled, back to a time when things were peaceful, before I knew of Michael's torturous arrival.

Chapter 40

Jacob walked into my apartment ahead of me, making sure the coast was clear before he'd allow me access. I shook my head. He was so cute!

Walking into my bedroom, I pulled out a large overnight bag and began rummaging through my dresser drawers to find suitable clothes.

"He seemed like a real jerk. Why would you stay with him?" Jacob's voice angrily threw a dart of hatred out.

"I don't know. I honestly don't know." I shrugged. For the life of me, I couldn't come up with a good answer. The more time went on, the less I remembered being happy with Michael. Not that everything was miserable, but the good times faded a lot quicker than the bad times.

"What was his problem?" Jacob fumed.

"He's always doing that. He has to control and manipulate every situation. He knows I'll never take him back, so he has to cause as many problems as he can with my life. He won't leave me alone. He can't let me be happy." I said sadly. "I'm really sorry about that."

"Sorry about what?" Jacob crinkled his eyebrows in confusion at me.

"I didn't want you to have to see that." My heart broke. I had never wanted Jacob to see me at anything less than my best. He was an angel, and I wanted to offer him the world.

"Don't worry about it. You're only human." Jacob smiled as he kissed my forehead again.

"Mew?" Marie Rose asked as she jumped up onto the bed.

"Oh my goodness! I completely forgot about you!" I scooped her up in my arms, burying my face in her soft fur. She began to purr.

"What are we going to do?" My eyes fell as I looked up at Jacob for sympathy. "She's too young to be left alone!"

"So we'll take her with us." Jacob smiled.

"Really?" My eyes lifted. "But what about Sera?"

"Sera will be recovering from surgery, and I'm sure Marie will be too scared to bug her. Where are her things?" Jacob set off in search of a cat carrier and the rest of Marie Rose's 'belongings'.

"She has canned food in the cabinets, her toys are in the living room, and her litter box is in the bathroom." I called out. "You're wonderful."

"Thanks. Uh… can you get her litter box?" Jacob cautiously replied.

"Sure." I laughed. With my darling kitty in my left hand, I resumed packing with my right hand. I could sense Jacob had returned. Glancing over my shoulder, he held up the carrier.

"There you go, baby girl. Don't worry. You won't be in there long." I sadly pushed Marie into her temporary prison.

"Rear!" She cried in protest, frantically pawing at the exit.

"I know, sweetie. It's not forever." I stuck my fingers through the slotted front door.

"Are you girls almost ready?" Jacob's voice was soft.

Scanning the bag quickly, I looked up at him.

"Yeah, I guess so." I nodded.

"Good. Let's get out of here." Jacob wrapped his right arm around my shoulder, and I pulled his hand towards my mouth.

"You're wonderful. Do you know that?" My lips echoed off his firm grip.

"So you keep telling me." He kissed the side of my head as he closed the front door to my apartment behind us.

Chapter 41

Jacob had decided to drop me off at the police station and return as soon as possible. He bravely had volunteered to help Marie Rose become acquainted with her temporary new home while I began the daunting task of filing police paperwork. Sergeant Saroka, who had originally tried to apprehend Michael, was there. He was not the person using a pen. His hand was bandaged severely from his dangerous dance with my ex just a few hours before.

I could hear my cell phone ringing. Quickly, I looked at the caller id. It was Alena. I muted it, and my attention returned to the papers. That is, until Alena called me immediately back.

"I'm sorry. Can I take this?" My cheeks burned with embarrassment.

"Sure, just make it quick please. The sooner we finish up this report, the sooner we can issue that arrest warrant." The cop's voice was monotone as he rambled off protocol.

"Hey baby. What's up? I'm in the middle of paperwork. Can't it wait?" I whispered rapidly into the phone.

"I just thought you should know baby girl. After you guys left, my car was the only one in the parking lot." Alena's voice was ice cold.

"Huh?" My brain couldn't wrap itself around what Alena was trying to say.

"Put me on speaker phone." She instructed. I followed her command.

"Okay, babe. You're on." I called out to her.

"After everyone left, my car was the only was in the parking lot." Alena repeated. Both of the police officer's heads perked up.

"I thought Michael said he brought his sister's sick cat there to receive medical treatment." The cops exchanged concerned glances.

"So then, what was he doing there?" I pondered aloud.

"What was he doing here with a knife on him, and no cat and no car?" Alena spat.

My heart sank as the slow realization of the truth came to the forefront of my mind. Michael had brought a weapon to my work as a last ditch effort to control my life. Simply put, he intended to control when my life ended.

"Thanks babe." I hung up as a chill froze me in my fearful place. I just looked at the cops with pleading eyes. In an instant, this situation had gone from a nightmare that I desperately awaited to wake up from to a hell I couldn't escape.

"That was Alena." I mumbled. "She's the office manager."

"Don't worry. We'll make sure every available unit is out there searching for him until he's apprehended." The cops' words were of very little reassurance. I smiled weakly at him.

Hey babe. I'm here. Where are you? Jacob texted me.

Interview room 3. I replied. *Ask the cop at the front if you can join us. You were there. You're a witness.*

A few moments later, Jacob walked in the room. I was still shaking from Alena's chilling revelation as I curled up into his arms.

"What's wrong babe?" Jacob squeezed me tightly.

"Alena said there wasn't an extra car in the parking lot. That after we all left, her car was the only one there." I pouted, shaking.

"Oh really?" Jacob's voice hardened as his body slightly stiffened. The logic train had eluded only me. Everyone else seemed to immediately interpret what Alena had truly meant by her words.

"Yeah." I whispered my reply.

"Did you tell the police?" Jacob spoke up. He made little effort to keep our conversation private.

"They're aware. I put Alena on speaker phone." I nodded.

"Sorry to interrupt, but we would like to you read over this statement, and if you're satisfied with it, could you please sign the bottom?" The cop pushed his papers and pen at me.

"I was a witness. Is there anything you'd like me to sign?" Jacob offered.

"Yes, sir. Could you please read the statement, verify its accuracy and sign it too?" The cop's face remained placid.

"Don't worry. We're going to catch him." Sergeant Saroka tried his best to be reassuring. I offered a half smile at him.

Once I had finished with the pen, I relinquished control over to Jacob.

"We'll be in touch. Is there anything else we can do in the meantime?" The cops stood up from the table, and we mirrored them.

"Can someone make sure Happy Pets is safe?" Jacob asked.

"Oh honey." I rolled my eyes.

"He brought a knife to your work. What makes you think he won't try something stupid again?" Jacob lectured.

I sighed, coming up empty with a reasonable retort. So I just shrugged.

"Will do." The cops nodded. "We'll send an officer by to make sure the other witnesses are alright."

"Come on babe. Let's go home." Jacob kissed the top of my head.

"You mean your home." I corrected.

"Home is where the heart is. As long as I'm with you, I'm home." Jacob smiled. My heart melted at his warm words, and the rest of my body began to smooth out the wrinkles stress had caused as Jacob and I began our journey "home".

Chapter 42

I could hear Marie Rose crying from the front entry. She sounded so miserable!

"Poor thing." I cooed.

"I didn't know what to do with her, so I left her in the carrier." Jacob shrugged helplessly. A boyish grin appeared on his beautiful lips.

"Are you serious?" My eyes lunged at him in disbelief.

"Yeah." Jacob sheepishly shrugged.

"You jerk!" I playfully smacked his arm, and his face lit up in amusement as his body flinched away.

"I'm sorry." He laughed as he fetched the kitten. I could hear her frantic claws desperately trying to operate the escape hatch.

"There you go, baby. Come to mama." I opened the front door, but Marie Rose wasn't interested in cuddling with me. As soon as she saw an opportunity, Marie shot out of her prison and ran around Jacob's house looking for a safe place to hide.

"Sorry." Jacob apologized again. As much as I wanted to smack him across the back of his head, I couldn't. He was just too darn cute!

"It's okay. I hope she'll forgive me." My shoulders slumped as my body dropped onto a couch. Once my brain had realized that the immediate ordeal was over, my body quickly burned through all of its adrenaline, leaving me exhausted.

"What a day." I exhaled loudly. My stomach growled at me, threatening to release a hellish wrath on me.

"Are you hungry?" Jacob's power of observation was astute. Raising my eyebrows in response, I just stared at him.

"What would you like to eat?" He flopped on the couch next to me and began rubbing my thigh.

"I have no idea. Food. Food sounds good." I laughed weakly.

"Long day, huh?" Jacob sympathized.

"You could say that again!" I nodded in agreement.

"Long day, huh?" Jacob grinned.

"You are such a dork!" I laughed, giving his arm a playful push.

"If you'd like, I can go out and get you anything you want to eat. That way, you and Marie can get settled in." He rubbed my arm.

"Okay. Are you hungry?" I asked.

"A little bit."

"Would you like to share a pizza?"

"Sure." He nodded slowly.

I stood up with the intention of retrieving my wallet. By the time I'd gotten back to the living room, Jacob had already left. I sighed, resuming my slumped position on the couch.

My mind was reeling from the day's events. I had continued on with my life. Why couldn't Michael? To my knowledge, I hadn't done anything to deserve his wrathful vengeance. Other than discontinue the relationship.

I heard a light tap at the front door. Every hair stood up on my head as "Fight or Flight Syndrome" made its second appearance today. Slowly, I tip toed over to the front door. I made a diligent effort to not make a sound, instead listening for any information that would tell me who had found me.

"Hello? Is anybody home?" Alena's voice called out.

My whole body visibly dropped a foot in relief. I commanded the locks to open with a twist of my fingers and quickly opened the front door.

"Come on in." I whispered, looking around in paranoia. Did anybody else know I was here? Had my safety been jeopardized, or was I imagining things?

"What are you doing here?" When I didn't see a single pair of eyes staring back at me, I closed the door and turned around.

"I told you I was going to bring Sera by after her surgery, baby girl." Alena shook her head in disbelief. "Are you okay?"

"Sorry. It's been a long day." I reached for the small bundle of fur that had been tenderly wrapped in a blanket. I could see a plastic shopping bag dangling from Alena's wrist. For a split second, I wanted to peer inside at its contents.

"Careful. She's still groggy from the anesthesia." Alena warned.

I spun the package around. Sera's pupils were enormous and unblinking. It was obvious that she couldn't focus her vision, or move any part of her body due to the knock out gas. Anyone looking at her could tell that physically she was there, but mentally, nobody was going to be home for awhile.

"Is she okay?" My heart pounded in fear for this furry friend.

"She'll be fine. We had to remove a couple of teeth so for the next week, I'd recommend only wet kibble." Alena reached over and lovingly stroked Sera's head.

I felt a sharp guilty repetitive stab in my heart as I looked into her eyes. She was scared, confused. She had no idea why her head was throbbing, or what had happened to her. Where was her daddy? And who were these strange people hovering around her? Were we to blame for Sera's misery?

She was exceptionally warm as I held her furry little body. She was motionless. Her unblinking pupils were dilated enough to absorb the whole room. And yet, the only thing she reacted to was daddy coming home.

"Hey! How's my sweet girl doing?" Jacob's face lit up as soon as their eyes met. Her small frame began to tremble with relief. Her front paws inched the air, trying to scoot closer to her beloved. Delicately dropping the pizza box on the living room table, his massive hands swooped in and rescued Sera from the clutches of the evil shrews that had inflicted all this pain onto her.

"Welcome back." I smiled. "Look who's here."

"I see that. I was wondering whose car was out front." Jacob smiled at Sera.

"Sorry I didn't call. It's very difficult to drive with a puppy in your lap." Alena smirked.

"How much do I owe you for the pizza?" I asked, fidgeting with my wallet.

"Don't worry about it." Jacob shrugged.

I tilted my head to the left, my eyes throwing disapproving daggers Jacob. He was oblivious though. I glanced at Alena, and she shrugged.

"Like I told baby girl, Sera had a couple of teeth removed. So only wet kibble for the next week, okay?" Alena lectured.

"Got it." Jacob nodded, still focused on Sera.

"And no more people food!" Alena and I cried in unison.

"Alright baby girl. I'm going to head home. Call if you need anything okay?" Alena wrapped her arms around me.

"Am I working tomorrow?" I asked as my arms instinctively clung to hers.

"Naaahh. Don't worry about it. Take a day to get settled in. Besides, Michael already showed up once. Until he's in police custody, I want to make sure you're safe. And he doesn't know you are here. So you can do God knows what." Alena grinned, her eyes motioning towards Jacob. I just shook my head, trying not to smirk.

"Take care, doll face." Alena gently petted Sera. She dropped the plastic bag on the living room table.

"Thanks again." Jacob called after her.

"Any time." Alena threw her words over her shoulder as her fingers guided the door back into its frame.

"So what kind of pizza did you get?" I stuck my hands in my back pocket and slowly sauntered over to the box. Jacob slowly sat down on the edge of the couch and gently placed Sera on his lap. If her vision decided to work, she'd have a grand view of the pizza box. Her nose responded to the delicious aromas it offered.

"Cheese. I wasn't sure what kind of toppings you liked." Jacob's voice was brisk and to the point. Glancing over, his attention in its entirety belonged solely to Sera.

"Mushrooms and green peppers." I replied, opening the box.

"Ew gross!" Jacob squealed as he crinkled his nose.

"Why? What do you like?" I challenged, delicately picking up a slice of gooey goodness.

"Pepperoni." He replied.

"Ew gross!" I laughed.

"Whatever! Pepperoni is a classic!" We shared a good belly laugh.

"Have you seen Marie?" I asked, looking around.

"Not since I let her out." Jacob shook his head.

"Okay." Quietly, I sat down on the other side of the couch. Neither one of them bothered to look over at me. I just nibbled my pizza in silence.

My thoughts began to drift back to the events that had unfolded earlier. Emotionally, I couldn't understand what had possessed Michael to do what he did. I had left him alone. Why couldn't he do the same? His actions had stripped away the false sense of security time had offered, leaving me vulnerable to all sorts of wild and crazy thoughts. Logically, I knew Michael was a controlling man, and he would stop at nothing to make sure he had the final say over what happened in my life. Thoughts swirled around viciously in my head. If only there was a way to beat him at his own game….

"Earth to Leslie. Are you there?" Jacob's fingers gently pushed my shoulders as I crash landed back to reality.

"Huh?" I blinked my eyes and turned to face him.

"You disappeared there for a while. Are you going to eat your pizza?" Jacob smiled at me.

"Sorry. Yes, I'm going to eat it." Looking down, I could see that the pizza slice had made its juices comfortable into my jeans. I crinkled my nose.

"It's been like that for 10 minutes." Jacob laughed.

"Wonderful." I wrinkled my face at him.

"The bathroom is down the hallway on the right." Jacob sensed my desire for warm and dry clothes. Nodding, I pushed myself off the couch. I grabbed my bag of clothes and made my way down the hallway.

Closing the bathroom door behind me, I took a breath and looked around at his drab decorations. *It's definitely a man's home*, I thought. *I wonder how he'd feel about adding a woman's touch…*

Wiggling out of my slimy jeans, I dug around in my bag for my favorite pair of flannel pants and a tank top. They had the logo of my favorite football team on them. I folded my dirty clothes into each other and left them in my hand. I didn't want to risk sliming my clean clothes by putting pizza pants in the bag.

With my goods in hands, I meandered down the hallway back to the living room.

"Do you have a bag I could put these in?" I asked.

"Wow. Don't you look good." Jacob's eyebrows rose.

"Oh, hush. I'm in my pajamas." I rolled my eyes.

"I have bags in the kitchen." He delicately moved Sera over to the middle cushion and led the way. I followed him in silence, watching as he opened a drawer and retrieved the desired item.

"Here you go." Jacob fluffed the plastic in the air. I dropped the gooey clothes in.

"You really do look cute." Jacob's hand rubbed my arm. It began to tingle where he touched.

"You're just saying that because you have to." I scoffed, inching closer.

"Oh yeah? Says who?" He challenged, raising an inquisitive eyebrow.

"It's in the rule book. You're my boyfriend. You have to think I'm cute." I laughed with a nod.

"Oh really? Is that so?" Jacob grinned at me, revealing those adorable crows' feet around his eye that I loved so much.

"Yep." I pulled at his shirt, silently beckoning him closer.

"You're so cute. Do you know that?" He leaned in.

"Maybe." I tossed the word out coyly. His only reply was a gentle kiss. I felt a ripple of joy vibrate up my sternum as a wave of goose bumps fled in the opposite direction. His lips were so soft against mine.

Slowly, Jacob pulled away from me. We stood a couple inches away from each other in silence, just taking in the moment. With a smile, I held the corner of my lower lip in my teeth. As I began to move my hands up towards his neck, his strong arms wrapped themselves around me like a snake moving in for the kill. I could feel their raw strength underneath the gentle exterior he wore for me. I didn't have to coax him very much to come back. It was as we were on the same unspoken psychic connection. His lips dove deeper into mine. I could sense a deep passion threatening to burst within our souls.

Jacob didn't pull his face away from mine, and I didn't retreat. His arms flexed around my petite waistline and his hand pressed against the small of my back, forcing my back to arch. His chest pushed firmly up against mine. His body was so warm. I could feel his heart thrashing wildly. The only response I could come up with was to clutch his neck tighter. I could feel the top of my scalp start to burn with a desire that Jacob controlled. My skin began to pulse as my heartbeat ran faster and faster. Was it me, or was the room getting significantly warmer? My fingers curled themselves around his hair, begging me to give them permission to rip Jacob's shirt off of his deliciously muscular body.

An ear piercing shriek shattered the moment. Jacob and I froze as we crash landed back to reality. Looking into his eyes, I could see that they were glazed over from our passionate encounter. I wondered what mine looked like.

"Let me go see what she wants." Jacob hung back for a second, then left. It took my foggy brain a minute to realize that the shriek we heard must've come from Sera. What kind of drug was Jacob to cause such a delightful fog?

Deep down in the pit of my stomach, I felt a strong ire towards Sera. *Thanks for ruining the moment.* I thought bitterly.

On the other hand, I bet he'd make a great parent someday…

Chapter 43

My blood pumped furiously at the memory of our intimate moment. In a daze, I wandered to the bathroom. I wondered if I had that "glow."

I stood in front of the mirror and smiled. My eyes sparkled. My cheeks were flushed. The Cheshire cat had left his grin upon my lips.

Making my way back down the hallway, I had abandoned the mirror in favor of resuming things between us. Now, where was that beau of mine?

I found him lying on his bed with Sera in his arms. Smiling, I laid down next to him.

"Howdy, stranger." I continued smiling at him.

"Hey." An ambiguous one word reply.

"How's Sera doing?" I scooted closer to Jacob.

"I'm not sure. I think the anesthesia might be wearing off. Do you know if Alena brought any puppy aspirin or anything over?" His forehead wrinkled with concern.

"I don't know. I can check if you want." I offered.

"Please?" Jacob asked.

"Sure." I pushed myself off of his firm mattress and aimed my feet towards the plastic bag Alena had left us. In the heat of the moment, I had forgotten about its existence. In fact, I had forgotten about a lot of things existing!

As I rummaged around inside the bag, I heard a maraca mimicking sound echoing from somewhere down at the bottom. My fingers wrapped around something small and slender as I pulled it to the surface.

My eyes told me it was the standard prescription bottle we used at Happy Pets. Spinning the cylinder around with my fingertips, I spied the label. Immediately, I knew it was a canine painkiller. As I began to remove the childproof cap, my gut told me to stop. *It's too soon after the surgery. The anesthesia needs to wear off a little, or else she'll throw it back up.*

I sighed, knowing my gut instinct was correct. Pushing the cap back on, I brought Alena's gift to Jacob.

"I got something a little better." I sat on the edge of the bed and pushed the prescription bottle towards him.

"What is it?" Jacob took his eyes off of Sera for a second.

"Canine painkillers. I think we should wait until she's not dopey anymore." I warned.

"How come?"

"For the same reason you're not allowed to eat or drink before undergoing surgery. The anesthesia can mess with a person's stomach, and I don't want Sera to throw up." I lectured.

"So, how long do we have to wait?" I had never seen Jacob's impatient side before. It didn't matter to me. Any side of him was cute!

"I'd say when she's coherent and can move on her own." Staring at Sera, anyone could see she was wobbly. It wasn't the fact that she couldn't walk or stand on her own. It would appear that she was having difficulty even holding up her own head!

"For now, I'd say just let her rest." I smiled, reaching for Sera's soft fur.

"Alright." Jacob sighed.

"So, where were we?" Smiling, I laid down and cuddled up to Jacob.

"Huh?" Blinking, he looked at me.

I just smiled seductively in response.

"I think we should wait until Sera's feeling better." Jacob smiled innocently back.

"Okay." My reply was brisk. Could he tell I was disappointed? I couldn't help but yawn.

"Looks like my other girl is getting sleepy." Jacob extended his left arm around my shoulder. I took a quick peek at Sera and I could see her eyes were closed, her small face still and peaceful on Jacob's chest. *That's actually a good idea, pup. I hope you don't mind if I borrow it.*

Curling up on the other side, I nestled my right cheek against Jacob's muscular ribcage. He was very warm and soft.

"I guess I'll see you in the morning then." I smiled up at him.

"Absolutely. I'm here if you need anything." Jacob kissed my forehead. "Get some rest. You've had a long and exciting day."

My libido immediately responded at the memory of what exciting events had transpired in his kitchen earlier. I didn't say a word. I just closed my eyes and drifted off to sleep while listening to his warm and caring heart beat.

Chapter 44

I surrendered to the realm of consciousness when the sunlight beaming
in through the window onto my face neared blinding stages. Arching my
back with my arms outstretched, I greeted the morning. I could feel
Jacob's arm still around my shoulder and I smiled. It was nice to know
that we had managed to sleep the whole night together while cuddling. I
peeked over and saw he was still sleeping with Sera. She was right where
I'd left her the night before, curled up on daddy's chest.

Very slowly, I raised myself up off of Jacob's bed. Since coffee was a
necessity, I decided to start my journey there.

I rummaged through the cabinets in search of the coffee grounds when
a familiar sound greeted me.

"Mew?" Marie asked, rubbing up against my leg.

"Well, good morning! And where have you been hiding all night?"
Gratefully, I scooped her up in my arms and began to scratch behind her
ears. Marie purred loudly, happily accepting human affection for the first
time.

"Well, good morning ladies. And how are we today?" Jacob smiled groggily at me. He was holding Sera in his arms. Her eyes glowed at the realization of a 'new friend', and her delicate nose began to furiously sniff the air. Marie stopped purring and retreated into my chest.

"I don't think Marie is too happy." I laughed as Marie drew her ears back and glared at Sera.

"Hopefully, she gets over it." Jacob shrugged. Marie wasn't about to 'play nice' so early in the morning. She leapt out of my arms, seeking solace in her mystery hiding spot instead.

"Where's your coffee, honey?" I asked, turning my attentions to Jacob. "I was going to make us a pot, but I couldn't find the coffee."

"I keep the grounds in the freezer." Jacob's left hand extended to the freezer door and gave it a hard yank. Bewildered, I stared inside to find a yellow container staring back at me.

"It helps keep them fresher longer." Jacob shrugged as I reached for the frosty container.

"How often do you make coffee?" I just stared incredulously at him.

"Not that often." Jacob laughed.

"Apparently not!" I shook my head at him. I could feel his massive hand on the back of my head as he ruffled my hair.

"Hey now! That was uncalled for!" My face scrunched together as if the vacuum of adolescence had sucked my morning spirit away.

"You're so cute when you pout!" Jacob laughed, kissing my forehead.

"I'm glad you think so." I still offered a scour in his direction. "Are you going to work?"

"I'm not sure. Are you going to be okay here?" Jacob's smile vanished; his beautiful face radiating concern instead of playful morning banter.

"I guess. I mean, I don't see why not." I shrugged. "Besides, I can always call if there's a problem, right?"

"Absolutely." Jacob wrapped his free arm around me in a loving embrace. Too bad we weren't the only ones involved!

"Ruff!" Sera protested. She began to wiggle, as if she desperately wanted to get out from our hug.

"Oh! I'm so sorry! You want to go out, don't you?" Jacob cooed. His attention had completely narrowed in on Sera. With a shrug, I went back to making that fresh pot in instant breakfast.

"I'll be right back." With a quick kiss, they vanished outside. I stood up on my tippy toes, eager to get a good view of Sera. The animal lover in me was curious to see her progress.

I could see Jacob squatting down as he tried to coax Sera to walk. She just sadly turned her head around to look at him. I could hear him talking to her. She only whined and whimpered in response.

Like a lost little girl, I palmed my cell phone. Any time there was a problem, I ran to Alena. Was it too early to be asking her advice?

Before I could make a decision, I heard Jacob and Sera walk back in the house. Correction. I could hear Jacob walk back in the house. I assumed Sera was in his arms.

"I don't understand." He shrugged.

"Is she hungry? Thirsty? Did you give her antibiotics and painkillers?" I asked any and every question that popped into my head.

"You know what? I hadn't thought about that. She probably hasn't had a drink since before the surgery!" Jacob rushed Sera towards her dishes with hopeful enthusiasm. Sera compromised, offering to imbibe a few sips of water.

"That's my girl!" Jacob smiled. Foolishly, he turned his back on her to retrieve her canine pills. Glancing down at her, I could see Sera staring straight at Jacob while she faithfully bent her hind legs. All I could do was pull my lips in and hope I didn't laugh.

"What's wrong? You look like you bit into a lemon." Jacob furrowed his brows at me.

I tilted my head repeatedly, nodding in Sera's direction.

"Sera Elizabeth!" Jacob scolded, patting her on her derriere. Sera didn't move. She just stared back at her daddy.

With a sigh, daddy and baby went back outside. I could tell he wasn't used to her antics. I just shrugged and drifted away.

My heart ached at the chaos that had become of my life. Alena's words replayed over and over in my mind. *My car was the only one left in the parking lot....* Even a blind person could see that Michael had intended on causing serious bodily harm. What I couldn't see was why. What had I done to him? Things between us had been over for nearly a year. Why couldn't he leave the past alone? I'd left him in the past, and I'd left him alone. Why was it such an issue for him to do the same?

Part of me worried that Michael would never stop playing these 'games', that I would never be free of him. Another part of me felt guilty. Jacob was such a great guy. He didn't deserve to be dragged into this nightmare. It wasn't fair of me to ask him to tolerate a war that was being waged, to bring feline bystanders to his doorstep. Why would he? Why should he? Jacob seemed so tolerant and understanding of this whole mess. *Maybe he could explain it to me*! I chuckled to myself.

"What's so funny?" Jacob asked. I spun around to face him, unaware that he'd come back in the house. He was on his knees, diligently working with a paper towel to clean up after Sera.

"Oh, nothing. Just thinking." I sighed with a shrug.

"Are you sure? You know you can talk to me." Jacob offered.

"I know." My eyes followed the sunbeams back to their source.

"So what's up?" Jacob repeated.

I didn't respond. I just stared out the window.

"Earth to Leslie. Are you there?" Jacob wrapped his hands around my waist, and I jumped.

"Geez! You scared the hell out of me!" My hand flew to my chest. I could feel my heart struggle to crawl down my throat and back into my ribcage.

"I'm sorry. I was talking to you. Didn't you hear me?" Jacob laughed, hugging me close. His body and the sunlight sandwiched me in a warm tortilla style hug.

"I guess not!" I laughed nervously.

"What's up? What's going on? Talk to me. What's on your mind?" Jacob said slowly.

"I don't know. I just…" I furrowed my eyebrows. I was having a hard time articulating what my heart had been talking about.

"It's okay. Take your time." Jacob smiled. My spirits invisibly expanded. There was something about his smile. It was warm, inviting, and absolutely captivating!

"I kind of feel bad." I pouted, my guilt flashing back in full force.

"Bad? About what?" His voice fluctuated with confusion.

"It's not fair." I whined.

"What's not fair?"

"To you."

"What's not fair to me?" He brain was still failing to board my logic train.

"This whole mess with Michael. I mean, here I am invading your house, and you're being so sweet about the whole thing." The corners of my mouth pulled downwards.

"Oh babe. It's okay. I don't mind." Jacob squeezed his arms.

"I know. But I feel bad. You have nothing to do with this. This isn't your battle." I hugged back.

"We're a team. We're in this together. Of course it's my battle. What kind of a boyfriend would I be if I sat back and let you deal with him on your own? I mean, he showed up at your work with a knife! You don't deserve that!" Jacob lectured.

"Maybe not, but you definitely don't." I retorted.

Jacob sighed and shook his head.

"What's the matter, honey?" I nuzzled my nose against his.

"What do you say about going to watch your football team this weekend?" Jacob's face lit up.

"Seriously?" My eyes popped open at the prospect.

"Why not? We don't need to deal with Michael's drama. Besides, maybe a mini vacation would be a good thing." His dimples waved enthusiastically at me.

"Okay. But what about Sera? And Marie?" Guilt had become a consistently faithful companion. I couldn't run off and play while one pet was recovering from surgery and another was hiding for her life.

"Why don't we have Alena house sit?" He offered a plausible solution.

"I don't know. I could ask her. Actually, I was thinking about seeing if she wanted to have lunch sometime this week." I admitted.

"Sounds like a plan to me." Jacob's arms loosened their loving embrace as Jacob's legs supported his weight.

"Where are you going?" I wrinkled my brows.

"I thought I'd get ready for work." With a kiss on the forehead, Jacob wandered off down the hallway, leaving me alone with a dog, a cat, and the rest of my thoughts that hadn't made it to the forefront of the discussion.

Chapter 45

"I'm telling you. That means something!" Sandy wrapped her lips around her straw and absent mindedly began to chew on the end. Alena and I locked eyes, sharing a bewildered gaze.

"I don't get it." My eyes darted back and forth between the checkered table cloth patterns at the café bistro, desperately trying to wrap my mind around the significance that Sandy claimed was right there in front of me.

"Baby girl, what are you babbling about?" Alena sighed, forcing her temper to remain under control. Nobody could find Alena's last nerve quite as fast as Sandy could.

"I think it's sweet that you two slept on top of the covers." Sandy smiled at me.

"Why is that?" I asked.

"It means that he cares about you for you, and not for certain things about you." Sandy replied with a smirk.

"But we already knew that, baby girl. Can we move on now?" Alena rolled her eyes. "So you were saying, Les?"

"I don't know, Alena. I'm just confused about a lot of things, I guess." I shrugged, staring into my ice water. Somehow, a lemon seed had managed to wriggle free of its yellow prison and float freely away into my water.

"Like what?" Sandy's words were sloppy. Glancing over, I could see that she had begun to drool as a result from chomping on her straw.

"I don't know. Just a bunch of stuff." I sighed.

"Take your time, baby girl. Start at the beginning and tell us what's going on. How are things with Jacob?" Alena stroked my right elbow.

"They're great! He's absolutely wonderful." I smiled. "This weekend, he wants to take me to watch a football game."

"Ew. Why would you want to watch football?" Sandy whined.

"Because I like football." I said slowly. "Jacob knows that. That's why he bought me front row tickets to see my favorite team play. Besides, Jacob thinks it'd be a good idea to get away from the area for a little while."

"Why is it a good idea to leave?" Sandy asked. Alena and I just glanced at each other, making sure we were sharing the same thought.

I swear, the wheel is moving but the hamster's been dead a long time...

"Because of what happened. Now, quit chewing on your straw." Alena

swatted at Sandy.

"You mean what happened with Michael?" Sandy's eyes gazed

innocently at me.

I sucked my lower lip inward and closed my eyes for a second. *Oh*

yeah. That hamster's definitely dead...

"Jacob thinks it'd be a good idea to get away for a couple of days. At

least, until the police catch Michael." I nodded slowly. I chose to focus on

keeping my breaths even. I didn't want to lose my temper. Sandy meant

well. She just partied too hard.

"I agree, baby. I can't believe he'd actually take things as far as he did!

I mean, did he try to contact you recently?" Alena's rubbing briefly

increased pressure. I could sense that the whole situation upset her.

"No! That's what is so strange. I hadn't spoken to him in months! The

last contact I had with Michael was six months ago. The judge told him to

stop calling me, stop trying to break into my house, and just leave me

alone. That's when I got the order of protection." My hands flew into the air, trying to grasp Michael's crazy thoughts as they wildly swirled above

our heads. *As if that were possible.*

"That's so weird." Alena and Sandy mumbled together.

"It is!" I nodded in agreement.

"Well, what else is going on baby girl?" Alena smiled at me.

"I don't know. I kind of feel bad for Jacob." The corners of my mouth

leaned downward to listen to what my heart what saying.

"Why?" Sandy piped up.

"I don't think it's fair that he has to put up with Michael's

shenanigans." My nose twitched with guilt.

"And neither should you. You've been leaving Michael alone to let him

live his life. You aren't harassing him. You have nothing to do with him.

He's trying to manipulate you into behaving poorly in front of Jacob.

Michael can't stand the fact that you found somebody new. That's why

he's trying to ruin it for you!" Alena spat.

"Really? You think so?" My eyebrows elevated ever so slightly at the

hope Alena had presented me. Was Michael really jealous? Was he that petty? Did Michael's neurotic need to control everyone and everything honestly have nothing to do with me? Was I truly innocent in this mess?

"Oh, absolutely! I think Michael knows that Jacob is a wonderful man, and that Jacob makes you happy in a way he never could." Alena nodded.

I smiled. "Thanks, babe. You're the best!" My arm reached around her shoulder as I squeezed a drop of loving happiness into her. I could feel the shackles that Michael's unexpected appearance had constrained my soul with, break free.

"Is there anything else bothering you baby girl?" Alena leaned into my shoulder and mildly squeezed back.

"Yes and no." I flopped my head left to right.

"Huh? How can it be both?" Sandy blinked at me. I watched her eyelids open, close, and then reopen. It didn't matter which phase I caught her in that process. Her eyes appeared to shine bright, as if the owner of the apartment upstairs had left every light on before vacating the property.

"Oh child, you have a lot to learn." Alena sighed as she rubbed her temple. "Keep talking, baby girl. What's on your mind?"

"I don't know. I'm just worried, I guess." I shrugged helplessly as my brain fidgeted with my heart. They didn't speak the same language, so translating was often difficult between the two. My brain spoke logic and my heart spoke the language of love.

"About Michael?" Sandy half smiled at me as she made a genuine effort to catch up to the same page as Alena and me.

"No, not that. I mean, besides that…" I stammered, shaking my head.

"Well, then what baby girl? What else is going on in there?" Alena's finger reached up and gently touched my forehead. *As if that was the source of my angst…*

"I don't know. What if things don't work out? What if Jacob thinks I'm a horrible person?" Doubt pulled the corners of my mouth downward.

"Why would he think that?" Sandy pondered aloud.

"Michael doesn't exactly bring out the best side of me." The left half of my face rose slightly higher than the right side as my left shoulder lifted in ignorant despair.

"Now you're just being ridiculous. Michael doesn't bring out the best side in anyone!" Alena snorted. "He's such a pompous jerk!"

"True. I'll give you that." My head bobbed up and down slightly.

"Is that it?" Sandy's face stared at me. I tried to read her expression, but she had no lines or muscle movements. It was as if she were a blank slate.

"You guys don't think things are moving too fast, do you?" My eyebrows scrunched together as they attempted to peer into the truth of the matter.

"How so?" Sandy mimicked me, trying to gaze with me.

"Baby girl, I think you're worrying for nothing. You're last relationship didn't work out so well, so you're afraid this one won't also. Jacob is a wonderful guy. You are truly lucky to have him. Quit worrying. You'll give yourself wrinkles for no reason." Alena raised an eyebrow at me as a warning.

"Are you sure?" I raised one back at her, trying to be funny.

"Most definitely. Don't get smart with me." I could see the corners of Alena's mouth threatening to leap upward as she fought back a grin.

"Yes mother." I scrunched my mouth together in a childish grin.

"But she's not your mom." Sandy's forehead wrinkled in confusion.

Alena and I just shook our heads together.

Chapter 46

Jacob and I rode in silence as his car zipped along the highway. I could hear his engine shifting gears as his foot roughly caressed the pedal. The tree line whizzed by us as the open air slapped my face with a variety of scents, both natural and unnatural. Glancing over at Jacob, I could tell he was focused on two things; the road in front of him, and the GPS at his side. I gazed back out the window, choosing to concentrate on the horizon.

I could feel a mix of emotions swirling around in my soul. I didn't understand why Jacob had insisted that we take a road trip to see a football game. Granted, I loved football. But didn't that mean he'd be missing a day of work? I couldn't help feel unworthy of such a sacrifice. I didn't ask Jacob to do that. He made that decision on his own accord, and yet, I couldn't help feel responsible. Jacob had chosen to take a road trip as a way to ensure my safety from Michael.

Michael… Just thinking about him made the blood in my veins turn into ice shards. What had possessed him to show up at my work with a knife? What was he really intending to do? I shivered as the cold hard truth stared me in the face.

"You okay?" Jacob frowned. Reaching over, his right hand lovingly stroked my left arm.

"Yeah." I smiled weakly at him.

"Do you want my jacket?" He sat up straight in preparation of removal.

"No thanks. I'm good." I shook my head.

"Making sure." Jacob kissed his fingers and then put them on my lips. That brought a real smile to my face.

Michael never would've done that, I thought sadly to myself. Taking in a deep breath, I retreated into my soul.

I wasn't sure why thinking about Michael made me sad and angry. It was kind of weird. I never thought fondly of him. It was as if my brain had either forgotten every good time. Or maybe there were none to remember.

What do you care about Michael for? That's in the past. Jacob is your future now. Don't you want a future with Jacob, or do you want to go back to Michael? My deepest subconscious whispered to me.

No! I thought viciously, shaking my head. Nothing could ever make me want to go back to Michael. Not after the love Jacob had shown me. Without question, he had taken me and Marie Rose into his home. He's always there to put a smile on my face. He offers me nothing but the utmost love and respect. Just thinking about how Jacob treated me, how it made me feel, made my spirit want to leap out of its epidermal manacles.

I glanced over at Jacob. He was still content concentrating on the road. I don't think it fazed him that the radio wasn't on or that we weren't conversing.

"How can you stand it so quiet?" My words broke the silence.

"I don't know. If it bothers you, you can put on the radio or something." Jacob shrugged.

"Does it bother you?" I asked.

"Not really. Does it bother you?" He tossed the question back at me.

"Kind of." I admitted.

"Okay then. What's up? What's going on? What's on your mind?" Jacob perched in his seat. His trance from the asphalt had been broken, at least for the time being.

"How come you wanted to go see a football game so badly?" I stared at him, imagining what his response would be. My gut hinted at avoiding Michael, but I wanted to hear what Jacob had to say.

"Honestly?" Jacob asked.

"Preferably." I laughed.

"I can't believe I found someone like you. It wasn't easy." I could see his beautiful dimples regally perched in his cheeks. There was a light in his eyes I hadn't noticed before.

"Huh?" I stared blankly at him, unable to process his words. *Whoa. Where did that come from?*

"Do you know how hard it is to find a truly good person in this day and age? It's nearly impossible! You love animals. You like sports. You are so sweet and kind, even to your ex who's a jerk. I am so lucky to have found you." Physically, his hand reached over to gently squeeze mine. But it was as if his love had been poured down my throat and cleansed my soul from the inside out. I sat there in silence, unsure of how to respond. I just stared at Jacob with my mouth slightly ajar.

"Well, say something." He laughed nervously. I could see his cheeks turning red.

"What do you want me to say?" I fumbled with my tongue.

"Say how you feel." Jacob offered his right shoulder up in ignorance.

"No, honey. I'm the lucky one." I smiled as my hand gently squeezed back.

Chapter 47

I picked at my hair, commanding various sections to turn and twist and salute a certain way. Running my hands over my shirt, I did my best to smooth out any wrinkles that were hiding within the folds of my shirt.

Looking in the mirror, I couldn't help but smile at the person staring back at me. My skin glowed; I was happy. The creases around my eyes that stress had held prisoner were now free, and my temples no longer pulsated from daily worries. The person smiling at me was in a good place, and it showed. I had found my best friend, my lover, my heart, my soul, my everything all wrapped up in the most glorious of packages.

Someone else's arms wrapped themselves around my waist as I felt a torso snuggle up against my back. I could see Jacob's face next to mine in the mirror, and we smiled at each other.

"You look great. I'm sure my mom will love you." His nose nestled against a little spot on my neck behind my right ear.

"That's easy for you to say! You're wonderful! What's not to love about you?! I'm the person dating her son. I have my work cut out for me." I laughed.

"Well I think you're absolutely wonderful, and anyone who knows you knows that's true." Jacob flexed his arms, and I could feel my body shift around the pressure being applied. "It's 5:37pm now, so we have a little under half an hour if we're going to make it to dinner on time." Kissing my cheek, he turned and left the bathroom.

I stared in the mirror, doing a quick mental scan of my appearance. My hand rose up, gingerly rubbing my jaw line. *If I'm going to meet his family,* I thought, *I suppose I should get rid of this five o'clock shadow…*

www.ingramcontent.com/pod-product-compliance
Lightning Source LLC
Chambersburg PA
CBHW022013010726
47494CB00003B/1012